BACK TO TITANIC

A TIME TRAVEL ROMANCE

LOVE THROUGHOUT TIME
BOOK ONE

ID JOHNSON

For Becky

CONTENTS

1

MILLIE

"HURRY UP, MILLIE." MY MOTHER FOLLOWS UP BY RAPPING ON THE bathroom door. "We're going to be late."

"We're not going to be late for anything," I answer. "We're on a ship. Nothing is going anywhere without us."

"You know what I mean. I want to go swimming before the pool is too crowded."

I open the door, shaking my head. "How am I supposed to swim in this thing? What's with all this extra fabric gathered at the waistline? It looks like I'm wearing half a parachute." Though, now that I see it, Mom's suit might be worse, looking like a prisoner's uniform with all the vertical stripes.

They're both pretty embarrassing.

"That's what ladies' swimsuits looked like in 1912." She straightens up my skirt as though I'm twelve, not twenty-two.

"Yes, but do we have to swim?" I ask. "Can't we just put on one of the gowns we bought and walk around the ship?"

"We'll have time for that later," she insists.

"She's not going to change her mind," my little sister, Ally, interjects. "Believe me, I've tried. I look ridiculous in all this embroidery, or whatever this is."

"At least you don't have a lump of parachute around your waist," I complain. "I swear, it's going to get filled up with water, and I doubt I'll stay afloat."

"I just hope no women were dressed like this when the original *Titanic* sunk," my sister says. "I'd hate to go out looking like this."

Mom looks at us both with a frown. "Girls, now, stop it. We agreed we were going to have fun on *Titanic 2*. Everyone's in period costumes. It's not like you'll be the only ones in the pool."

As usual, I cave at the pleading look in her eye. She's been waiting for this trip all year. "Okay, I'll do this for you... and because this ship is actually pretty cool. It looks just like the movie, which of course I've memorized after we re-watched it at least a dozen times this past week. But as soon as we're done swimming, I'm getting out of this thing."

"All I'm asking for is a few pictures." Mom's satisfied smirk has me shaking my head as she hands me another hunk of material. "Don't forget the scarf. It's a very important feature of the outfit."

"Wow, more fabric," my sister groans, taking hers. "I'm sure glad we were born in this century."

"Be lucky you won't be wearing corsets with the gowns later," Mom continues. "Those were so constricting, the women had a hard time eating much in public." She waits while I adjust the scarf, which is closer to a hat and is definitely going to fall off in the water. "You two look wonderful. Let's go enjoy ourselves."

"I really will try." I mean it.

Ally giggles. "When you first mentioned a cosplay cruise, I was thinking Disney princesses." She holds up her hand before Mom can answer. "But this is fun, too."

She opens the stateroom door just as two women are walking by —in bikinis.

"Mom—"

"Okay, maybe not everyone is in period costumes, but most people will be, I promise." She gives us a labored smile.

"Right." I just want to get this over with. I'll do a lap or two, take a picture, then I'm marching right back up here to change into something that actually flatters my curves.

"You're lucky to be in the twenty-first century for a lot of reasons," Mom says as we walk up the stairs toward the upper deck. "The pool here on *Titanic 2* is outside on the top deck, and of course, we can swim in it whenever we want. On the original *RMS Titanic*, the pool was indoors, on F Deck. Women could only swim there during their designated women-only time."

"I'm not surprised since it was over a hundred years ago, but it sounds tedious," Ally chimes in. "There were way too many stupid, pointless rules for women."

I nod, watching a couple walk by in outfits that look exactly like the lead couple in the movie. "I'm so glad I don't have to live with any of that old-fashioned sexism."

"Class difference was an issue as well," Mom continues. "You couldn't even get near the pool if you weren't a first-class passenger. Oh, I think of those poor people in steerage. They were actually locked down below while the first-class passengers got onto the lifeboats. I can't even imagine the terror."

"Just the idea gives me a chill," I say. "Everyone is a human being who deserves to live. I can't believe things were like that back then."

"We know it's true, though, from all the documentaries we've watched with Mom on the subject, as well as things she's learned from research," Ally says. "You're a real wealth of historical knowledge, Mom."

Mom grins as she opens the glass doors and we step out onto the deck, which smells like a mix of chlorine and salt air, with a tad of burning fuel mixed in. The skyscrapers of New York City are starting to fade into the distance now as we head farther out to sea.

I'm so glad I don't get seasick.

"At least a lot more people are in period costumes up here," I say. "I still feel ridiculous, but at least I'm not alone."

Ignoring me, Mom takes a deep breath. "Doesn't it feel wonderful, breathing the fresh ocean air?"

Did she not smell the diesel?

Apparently not, because she keeps talking. "Now, this ship is a lot larger than the original *Titanic*, but it's kept its charm, don't you think?"

"Yeah, sure, but—"

My eyes lock with a man standing on the other side of the pool. Even from this distance, I can see his bright blue irises, the color of the sky. His face is chiseled and attractive, with a strong jaw and sandy blond hair. Even in his period-appropriate men's bathing suit, which just looks like bike shorts and a tank top—lucky him—I can see every well-defined muscle.

"Millie?"

"I'm sorry. What, Mom?"

"Where did you go there?" she asks, but she doesn't wait for an answer. "Anyway, as I was saying, this ship is larger by ten thousand gross tons. But that was necessary. Of course, they had to add all the modern safety features and upgraded engines, so that took up a lot of room. You know, they first started building this ship in 2012, so they had to do a lot of work before we got to finally be on her maiden voyage today."

I look away from my mom and crane my neck to find the man again, but no luck.

"And now here we are, heading to Southampton! It's a reverse course from the original *Titanic's* maiden voyage," she says as I turn back to see her smile. "So, let's make the most of it."

"There's a table over there." Ally points near where the man was standing.

I still don't see him anywhere. There's something about him....

"Let's claim it before someone else does," Mom suggests.

I nod. "Even though it seems like I could shove my phone... or even my entire purse into the parachute on my waist, I don't want it to get wet, so we might as well put our stuff somewhere safe."

"Do you think this will be safe with all these people around?" Ally asks. "I have my whole life on this phone."

"Same." I could probably recover most of it from the cloud, but not when I'm stuck in the middle of the ocean with no way of getting a new phone.

"I'll watch our things while you two swim," Mom says. "When you're done, you can watch my stuff."

"When I'm done, I'm going to go change," I argue. But that sounds selfish the minute it comes out of my mouth. Mom deserves this trip, and I'm going to help her have a good time. "But sure. I'll hide under a towel or something while you get a turn."

"You're so silly." Mom laughs a little, so much her eyes light up. I haven't seen that side of her much since Dad passed away, and it reminds me to help her enjoy what she loves. And boy, does she love the *Titanic*.

"Silly Millie." Ally wiggles her brows up and down, and I just shake my head. It's like we're kids again.

"Well, if we're going to go swimming, let's just go swim." I notice the women in bikinis are already in the pool, completely unobstructed by the inconvenient clothing of the early twentieth century. But then again, most others are in suits like mine, so on this cruise, they're the ones who stand out.

"Not before I get a picture of you both by the pool," Mom insists.

Great. Now the whole horrible outfit is going to be preserved for posterity. At least Ally will be in the photo, too, though her suit is almost cute next to mine.

"Go stand next to it, but wait before you jump in so your suits are still dry in the shot." She waves us toward the pool while getting out her phone.

"Okay, but hurry up, Mom," Ally says. "The water looks great."

We move over toward the pool and stand near the edge, turning toward Mom.

"Better smile," Ally says. "You know she won't take it if we're frowning, and we'll never get to swim."

I nod, pasting on a toothy grin.

Mom shakes her head. "I want to get the buildings in the city in the background. Scoot over to your right."

We shuffle over together. "Is that good?" I ask.

Mom checks her phone and frowns. "Not quite. Now you're both too close to each other. Millie, take a small step back so I can see all of Ally's swimsuit."

A deep sigh escapes my lips. "Okay."

I feel the slick concrete just a second too late to stop my foot, which slides back. I almost grab Ally for balance but force myself not to, my protective big-sister instincts kicking in.

Screaming, I feel the force of the hard cement on the top of my head, then the feel of the cool water rushing over my shoulders.

The world blurs quickly and turns black all around me.

2

Millie

"Ow." I reach my wet hand up to my head as it throbs, and sharp pains shoot through the top.

"She's waking up."

"Mom?"

But it can't be my mom. The person who spoke was definitely a man. More strange voices surround me, all of them male.

"Where did she come from?"

"I have no idea. I didn't see any women in the room."

"Make room, gents." This voice is deeper, somehow softer.

I open my eyes, and the first thing I see is bright blue eyes, the color of the sky.

Why is that familiar?

But everything else is blurry, so I blink a few times. My head is still pounding.

"What the hell is a woman doing in here?" This voice is gruff, harsh.

"Language, Remington. The lady is awake."

"She's no lady if she's in here during men's swim."

Swim—that's right. I fell in the pool. The bang must have been me hitting my head.

Finally, the blur fades, and bending over me is the handsome man I saw at the pool.

Or is he? He has the same handsome, chiseled features, but his hair is a shade lighter, and he's not in a swimsuit. He's fully dressed in a *Titanic*-era men's suit, but it's soaking wet. I guess he jumped in and pulled me out. I can still hear the water splashing around beside me. He must be someone else, but he looks so much like that man I saw earlier.

"Make room, lads," he says calmly. "Miss, are you all right?"

"I-I think so," I say. "But my head—"

He nods and waves all the men back.

I frown when he moves to the side, and I see a ceiling above me. "Why is there a roof?"

"What's that now?" He looks up and back down at me. "We're in the pool room, Miss, F Deck on the RMS *Titanic*."

"RMS—" *Titanic 2* doesn't have that in the name.

"The woman is crazy," the gruff man snaps. "She has no idea where she is, and she wandered into a men's swim. Scandalous."

More voices come from every direction.

"She's probably from steerage. Those people are like that. No doubt trying to find a man of means."

"I bet you're right."

"The security around here is atrocious. I'm complaining to the captain immediately."

The kind, handsome man talks to me again. "I think you should get to the doctor right away. But I believe we're going to need to carry you up there." All the men around him back away as if they're allergic to me.

What is wrong with these people?

"Well, looks like *I'm* going to need to carry you," he amends. "Perhaps I'd better properly introduce myself first. My name is Will Stewart."

I just nod, not quite ready to do much more talking yet, especially around all these angry men.

"Are you comfortable with me taking you to see the physician?" he asks. "I'd better get to you D Deck to see Dr. O'Loughlin right away. I need to warn you, though, it is quite a jaunt."

I could have a concussion, so I'd better get checked out. I nod again. I can't say I'm going to hate having this guy carry me anywhere.

He slides his arms under me gently, one at my shoulders and the other under my knees, and scoops me up in his arms like I weigh nothing. Just about everyone in the crowd of men is still grumbling as we pass, and their faces are full of scorn. I've never seen a group of people so angry about having to help someone in an emergency.

Several of them are still complaining about a woman in the pool for some reason, and every one of them is dressed in period costumes, most in swimsuits but a few in formal looking suits. I guess they're really intent on sticking with the role playing.

Even though we're both soaking wet, it feels good being in Will's strong, protective arms. It doesn't seem to matter that everyone else is mad at me anymore, especially once we've passed them all. He opens the door with his back and gently pulls me with him before it closes behind us.

It's more relaxing without all those mean men around, and I finally find my voice. "Your clothes," I say, nodding toward his drenched suit. "Why are you dressed in a suit by the pool?"

He chuckles lightly, and it rings in the air like music. God, even his laugh is gorgeous. "I wasn't there to swim," he explains. "I was just taking a tour of the pool facilities."

"How did the pool get inside?" I ask.

He frowns. "You must've hit your head pretty hard. The pool was built inside that room. Where else would it be?"

That's not right. Why would he try to confuse me? He seems so nice. "No, it's outside on the top deck. The sun was in my eyes."

"Miss, you must be confused due to head trauma," he insists. "Maybe you're thinking of another pool."

I shake my head. "No, the one on *Titanic 2.*"

"Two?" he asks.

I nod as we walk by a woman who's holding hands with a young boy. Both are in perfect period clothing. She gasps and covers the boy's eyes as we walk past, and she hurries in the other direction.

That's odd.

"Can you tell me how you ended up in the water, miss?" he asks, seemingly not noticing the woman and the boy.

"My mom was taking a photo, and I stepped back," I explain. "I guess I slipped."

"There were no other women in the room, certainly none with camera equipment," he replies.

"She was using her phone." More people pass, and not one of them is wearing regular clothes. At least there were a few people on the deck around the pool before I fell in who weren't taking everything so seriously..

"Phone?" He crinkles his brow. "Goodness, this is serious," he adds with a whisper. "You seem to be very confused. Can you tell me your name?"

"Millicent Baker." More people pass, all in period clothing. Most seem to overreact to us, which I find odd. I guess it's because his suit is all wet. "Everyone calls me Millie."

"Well, Millie, it's a pleasure to meet you, though the circumstances are less than ideal," he says. "Worry not. We'll get to the bottom of this soon," he says. "Dr. O'Loughlin is good at what he does, I'm told. He's the ship's surgeon and very experienced."

He's said the name before, and it dawns on me why it's so familiar. "O'Loughlin was on the original *RMS Titanic.*" With Mom's obsession about the ship, I've heard the name more than a few times.

"Yes, he's here on the *Titanic.*" He takes a light breath and looks at me. "I'd better pick up the pace."

He does just that, holding me a little tighter as he breaks into a jog. I lock my fingers together behind his neck to hold on tighter. Now that we've picked up speed, the breeze is giving me a chill, though the parts of me that are making contact with him are warm, and I feel pleasant tingles inside from his closeness.

Closing my eyes, I relax a little in his arms. My head is still throbbing, but I'm having fewer of those sharp pains. I want to find my family. I don't understand why they weren't right there with me. "Can you find my mother, please? Her name is Isabelle Baker. My sister, Allison, is also on board. They were right there with me when I fell in."

He shakes his head. "You must be confused from the fall. There were no other women in the room at all."

"I don't understand why they would leave me," I say. "They saw me hit my head and fall into the pool. I must've hit it on the corner of the other side of the pool when I slipped backward. We were just taking a picture."

"Maybe they were afraid they'd get in trouble." He shrugs his shoulders but keeps up the jog, turning toward a flight of stairs. We descend a flight or two. I can't really keep track. My head is swimming.

"Why would they get in trouble?"

"It was the men's swim time, Millie," he says as we turn a corner.

"But—"

"We're here." He cuts me off as we reach the doctor's office, and Will bursts through the door.

An older man with a big mustache comes forward. "What's the trouble here?" He looks at Will with a crinkled brow as if he's doing something wrong.

I'm so confused. The man is in old-fashioned clothes with a hat something like a ship's captain, and he looks a lot like the photos of the *Titanic* doctor I've seen in Mom's documentaries. A nurse runs in behind, complete with the triangle hat, floor-length long-sleeved dress, and a white apron. I look around and there's not a single piece of digital equipment in the room. In fact, everything looks fairly rudimentary, yet it gleams like it's all brand new.

Something's wrong here. This all looks too real. The *Titanic 2* is a close replica, but it was modernized. Surely, the doctor's office would have all the right equipment. What if an emergency happens out at sea? All this play-acting is going a little too far.

If that's what it is....

"This girl nearly drowned," Will explains quickly.

"Lay her here." It's clear he's the doctor. "Why on earth was she in the pool? It's not even noon. The women don't have it until two o'clock."

"I don't know." Will looks at me with his brow furrowed again as she sets me down gently.

I feel a chill when he steps away.

He seems to be concerned, while everyone else is mad at me for some reason, even the doctor. All I did was slip and fall.

"Well, you'd better see to your clothes, son," Dr. O'Loughlin says. "I'll take it from here."

Will looks at me with those bright blue eyes. "You'll be fine," he assures me. "The doctor will help you. I'll tell someone about your family."

I nod and watch him walk out the door, my heart sinking as he closes it behind him. I look back at the doctor and nurse, and neither of them is checking my blood pressure or helping me in any way.

I don't know what's going on, but it certainly doesn't feel like I'm going to be fine.

3

Will

I leave the infirmary and close the door behind me, taking a deep breath. I really don't want to leave Millie there. She seems so confused, lost, and vulnerable. And the way she seemed to melt in my arms as I carried her, I didn't want to let go. The strange things she had said keep echoing in my mind.

"Can I assist you, sir?"

"Hm?" I turn to see a crew member looking at me with a crinkled brow. I suppose I need to remedy these wet clothes. "No, thank you. I was just heading back to my room."

"Very well, sir." He doesn't look convinced, but he walks away.

I take another look at the door, wishing I could go back inside and check on her welfare, but it's too late for that. I certainly can't intrude now while she's undergoing an exam. Nevertheless, I can't help the nagging concern that I should do more for her.

Reluctantly, I head back to my room. My brother isn't in, and I don't hear my sister next door. I suppose they went to get some fresh air, so I'll have to go search the promenade for them..

I can't help running everything Millie said through my mind again as I change into a fresh, dry suit. Taking pictures with phones, the pool outside—such strange things to say. What's more curious is how she didn't seem to be dazed at all when she spoke of such things. When she first awoke, it was clear her head injury had left her confused, not as we approached the doctor's office, she seemed lucid. Except for her comments.

She clearly had an American accent, but it was like none I'd ever heard before. Plenty of Americans make their homes in Southampton, yet none have quite the same manner of speaking as I'd heard from Millie. Perhaps she's from one of the western states. With a country so vast, surely the accents vary.

Finishing up, I head out and begin to search the promenade for my siblings. Eventually, I track them down. Lounging in chairs with drinks in their hands, they look perfectly content.

"Will, how was the tour?" my brother, Edward, asks. "I can't say it wouldn't be a thrill taking a swim on a moving ship." He looks at the couple next to him. "Oh, how rude of me. Will, these are the Ryersons. Arthur, this is my brother, Will."

"Pleasure," Arthur says as I shake his hand and nod to his wife. "As I told Edward, my man here will be happy to get you a drink, if you'd like one."

I settle into the chair next to my sister, Agatha, while Arthur's liegeman steps over to ask what drink I'd prefer. "I'll have a brandy," I tell him.

"Yes, sir."

"Thank you," I say to Arthur, who nods and returns to his book.

I turn to Edward. "I can't say I'd ever want to go back to that pool again."

My sister frowns at me. "Why not? On a ship like this, I'd imagine it's lovely."

"It was dreadful." I take the drink from the man and give him a nod as he returns to his post near the Ryersons.

"I find that hard to believe," Edward says. "I'll have to take a look at it later."

"Mm." I shake my head, swallowing my sip. "It's not the facilities. Those are exceptional. It's the trouble that arose there."

"Trouble?" Agatha's forehead crinkles in confusion.

Edward lets out a chuckle. "My dear brother, what trouble have you caused?"

"None, I assure you." We're not the wealthiest family aboard, though we are well off enough to have purchased First Class tickets. Nevertheless, we are relatively young and inexperienced. Some might feel it necessary to judge us because of our ages, so I wouldn't do anything to draw overt attention to ourselves... not on purpose, anyway. "I had to dive in after a woman who nearly drowned."

Arthur and his wife look up at me, and Agatha places her hand on her chest. "You rescued a drowning woman?" she asks.

"I have a pile of soggy clothes in the room to prove it."

"But how on earth—no women are allowed in the pool room at this hour," she insists. "It's quite improper." Since our parents passed away three months ago, Agatha has taken it upon herself to keep us toeing the line socially. I suppose it's her way of honoring their memory. Our mother valued her social circles.

"And yet, there she was." I take another long sip of brandy.

"The women's swim session is at two o'clock" She sweeps back a stray strand of her light blonde hair. "What kind of a woman has the gall to slip into the pool when men are swimming.... My God, what was she wearing?"

I swallow before answering. I'm going to need another drink. "Ladies' swimming apparel."

"Goodness, she was half naked," she says, shaking her head. "And you had to carry her out?"

"Well, I couldn't very well let her drown. It was an emergency, Agatha." All I can do is shrug.

"I suppose." She takes a sip of her tea. "I hope the crew got her out of there immediately."

"I should say so," Arthur chimes in. I notice his wife nod in agreement.

"Actually, I carried her to the physician," I explain.

Edward brushes a hand through his sandy blond hair and chuckles again. "You carried the woman in swim clothes all the way to the doctor?"

Once again, my shoulders nearly touch my ears. "No one else was offering as much. She'd hit her head and was saying odd things, so I hurried her out for medical attention."

"Odd things?" Edward asks.

"She seemed to be confused about where she was," I explain. "And she was looking for her mother and sister, but there were no other women in the room."

"I agree. That is odd." Edward looks out to sea and takes another sip of his drink.

"Obviously, the woman is an absolute loon," Agatha decides.

A twinge of defensiveness rises in me, and I feel like speaking up in Millie's defense. But I hold my tongue. It makes no sense to defend the honor of a woman I barely know.

"It's positively frightening, thinking there's someone like that roaming around the ship unchecked," she adds. "The idea of her sneaking into the men's swim is just outlandish!"

"I'll be sure to ask about security," Edward adds. "I hate to think the captain is so lackadaisical that he wouldn't have guards at the doors to protect the swimmers from lunatics."

I think he might be poking fun at my sister for her outrage, but it's difficult to tell. Guards? Is that necessary? I think not. His comments do not help calm my protective feelings for Millie. In fact, I only want to defend her more, so I decide to quickly change the subject. "So, what have you two been up to while I was on the tour?"

"Ah, we've been on a bit of a tour of our own," Edward explains. "It's quite a fascinating ship. Seems there's no end to finding new things aboard her."

"And I've been reviewing the new schedule of ladies' activities." Agatha picks up the thick paper from her lap and waves it. "I'm quite interested in the new book club that is starting soon. It will certainly pass the time. And I've so enjoyed the afternoon tea in the library. It's a lovely room."

"I'm glad you're enjoying the voyage," I say, though I'm only half listening as my mind wanders back to Millie.

"We might as well make the most of it." She drops the paper and looks out to sea longingly.

I pat her on the arm. "Starting over isn't easy, I know. But Grandad's letter is very optimistic about America."

"Will and I are needed to help run his company," Edward reminds her.

"I know." She lets out a deep sigh. "I've read all the letters. It does sound like they have a lovely home. It just feels like I'm leaving so much behind. I don't know what people will be like in America. I've heard stories…."

"I'm sure the people in our grandparents' circle are lovely," Edward insists. "Grandmother is very happy there. It's quite evident in her letters."

"She had quite the social calendar back in Southampton," I add. "If she's found an acceptable community in New York, I'm certain there are fine people there. Don't fret. You'll fit right in."

"Perhaps." She takes another sip of her drink, and my mind goes back to Millie once more. I can't get over how certain she was that the pool was outside. I look around the promenade and can't imagine where that would be. Outside, it would be terribly difficult to control who was in the pool, and surely the ladies wouldn't want to swim beneath the gawking eyes of the men who might be passing by..

It's all just so odd.

"Will?"

I snap out of my thoughts and look at Edward. "I'm sorry?"

"Goodness, Will," he says. "Didn't you hear me? Are you sure you're all right?"

"I'm fine," I insist. "Just a little shaken from all the excitement, I suppose." I wave the steward over. "Another brandy, please."

"Right away, sir." He takes my empty glass and hurries off.

"You're drinking another?" Agatha asks. "It's almost time for the midday meal. I was hoping you'd escort me for a walk around the promenade before then."

"I'll take you for a walk," Edward says, standing and reaching out his hand to help her up. Another steward passes and takes his glass and her teacup. My brother looks down at me. "We'll be back shortly."

I nod. "I'll be waiting."

"Do stay here and come to eat with us," Agatha pleads. "It's where we'll get the best dinner invitations. I'm hoping to run into the Countess of Rothes again. She's quite lovely, and I'm hoping to dine with her and her family. Not that we have any control over where we are seated."

"Perhaps you should befriend some of the American passengers," Edward suggests. "That way, you can continue to have social engagements with them once we've settled."

"I'm happy to have correspondence with a woman as wonderful as the Countess, though she's certainly not American, brother." Agatha narrows her eyes at Edward..

The steward comes by and hands me my new drink. "Thank you," I say as he nods and hurries off.

Edward shrugs. "Well, you can't say I didn't try. Perhaps tomorrow you could make some new connections that will help us once we get settled."

"Perhaps," she says. "I just don't have the energy today."

He chuckles. "Very well." Edward offers his elbow, and she loops her arm through. He takes another glance at me. "We'll be back shortly."

"Take your time." I watch them walk down the promenade, turning to face the ocean after they've gone some distance. Millie hasn't left my mind. In fact, I've thought of her more as I've been in the outside air. She was so convinced about all the strange things she said, I hope she doesn't have any permanent damage to her mind.

Even soaking wet, I caught the light fragrance of her unique perfume. It seemed floral scented, but that flower must be exotic as it's nothing I've ever encountered. Even through my wet, somewhat chilled suit, I could feel her warmth. It was so hard to set her down on the doctor's exam table. I even felt a chill as I stepped away from her.

I stand, stepping out to the railing and gazing at the miles of ocean stretching before us. The fresh, salty air mixes with the oily, slightly sulfur scent of the steam engines, yet her perfume still haunts my mind.

I'm not going to relax until I know she's safe and well.

Spinning around, I leave my half-empty brandy glass with the nearest steward.

"Will?" Edward calls after me. "Where are you going?"

"I have to check on her," I explain as they hurry over.

"Her? The girl?" Agatha puts her hand on her cheek in shock.

"Yes." I look at Edward, who nods.

Understanding crosses over his face. "Well then, we're going with you," he insists.

I head toward the infirmary without another word, hearing their footsteps behind me.

4

Millie

"Well, then, let's have a look," the doctor says. The nurse steps in behind us and stands back to observe.

"What's your name, miss?" he asks as he starts examining me.

"Millie Baker." It's odd the way Dr. O'Loughlin seems to avoid touching me, letting the nurse take hold of my head and move my hair out of the way while he examines it. Neither of them have taken my blood pressure or my vitals the way my doctor does when I come in even if it's just for a check-up..

It's all so weird. I have this strange sensation that I'm out of place. Maybe it's just the bump on my head.

"Okay, Miss Baker, tell me how it happened," he says. "And how are you feeling? Any dizziness?"

I stop for a minute to consider his question. "Nope, no dizziness," I tell him. "At first, I felt a sharp pain, and my head was throbbing too, but now I'm not noticing that at all."

He smiles warmly. "Well, I think we have nothing to be too concerned about. There's a slight bit of bleeding, but nothing to fret over. I'll have Violet bandage this up, though you don't have to keep it on long, just until the bleeding stops... perhaps a few hours."

His tone is friendly, reassuring, and seems more empathetic than any of the doctors I've been to recently. Still, it's really weird that there aren't any modern instruments in the room. I guess they're trying to stay authentic to the time period. There's even a calendar on the wall that says it's April 10, 1912.

"Do you keep all your digital equipment in the cabinets or something?" I ask.

His smile falters a little. "How do you mean?"

"I'm just saying.... I don't see any of the modern equipment I usually see at the doctor's office." I watch the nurse, Violet, as she takes gauze and some very old-fashioned looking scissors out of a drawer, along with some cotton and a bottle of something.

The doctor tilts his head a little in confusion, but he smiles again. "I assure you, we have the most modern equipment available. Thankfully, we won't be needing it as I'm quite sure you'll be just fine."

The antiseptic scent is strong as Violet applies it with a cotton ball.

"Mr. Stewart said you had family aboard," the doctor says.

"Yes, my mom and sister," I say. "Can you find them, please? My mom is Isabelle Baker, and my sister's name is Allison. If I had my phone, I could just call them, but I left it with my mom."

He crinkles his brow. "Your mother has a telephone? She must be at home then?"

I shake my head. "No, she's here on the ship." *What is he talking about?*

"Well, then, it wouldn't be possible to telephone her," he says, still looking at me like he thinks I'm crazy. "We could send a telegram to anyone back home, but it wouldn't be possible to telephone her if she's on the ship."

"Tele—" I frown. What the hell is wrong with him? Is he pretending that cell phones don't exist even in an emergency. "Okay, but seriously. No, we can just call her cell phone. I know we're all pretending like it's the olden days or whatever, but this is kind of an emergency."

"Cell phone?" he asks, though he doesn't wait for my answer and ignores my pleas to just let all this cosplay shit go. "Perhaps I should keep you here to observe a bit longer. I'm confused. Is she on board or at home?"

"She's on the ship. Our room number is B-49, if that helps." I'm starting to get a bit irritated, and that antiseptic Violet put on my head is beginning to sting.

"Ah, she's in first class," he says. "I suppose that's what you meant by a phone. Those rooms all have telephones, but only for–."

"No, I—"

"We can send a steward to your room to fetch her." He steps forward to examine the bandage on my head. "Excellent work, Violet. Okay, Miss Baker. I'll see if—"

"Doctor!" A man calls out for him and bursts open the door at the same time.

"One moment." Dr. O'Loughlin steps over to a man dressed like a steward. He has an older woman leaning against his arm, and she looks like she's in pain.

"What's the problem here?" I overhear the doctor ask.

"This woman slipped on the stairs," he explains.

"Have a seat over here." The doctor directs the woman to a similar bed to the one I'm situated on. Turning back to the steward, Dr. O'Loughlin says, "I'll take it from here." The steward nods and turns to walk away. "Oh, and run up to room B-49 and have Mrs. Baker come see about her daughter here."

"Yes, sir." The steward hurries off, and Dr. O'Loughlin turns his attention to his new patient.

Violet looks at me. "You can take a seat out in the outer area. There are chairs out there. I need to go see about this woman."

"Sure thing," I say. "Thanks a lot." She nods at me with a weird look on her face and steps away to join the doctor. I touch my head, which has a bandage wrapped around like a headband. Hopefully, that's coming off soon. I step out of the main hospital area, but instead of sitting in the chair, which looks comfortable enough, I look around a bit.

"Well, it looks like you've sprained your ankle," the doctor says to the woman he's working on now.

I can tell the doctor and nurse are busy, so I pull a couple of drawers open and look inside quickly. Nothing inside looks modern at all. *What is with this place?* Everything is so old-fashioned, but it's sparkling clean, not rusted or tarnished like I've seen in museums. Are these all replicas or something?

Looking back up at the calendar, I can't help but think about how ominous the date is. It's just a few days before the original *RMS Titanic* sank. I wonder why they're pretending it's days before the sinking. Seems kind of morbid to me.

It would have been better to set things up as the actual day.

This is all so strange.

I've just pushed a drawer shut when the door opens, and I step away quickly. The same man who helped the woman inside is back, and he's almost out of breath. He frowns a bit as he looks at me.

"Doctor?" he calls out, and Dr. O'Loughlin—or the doctor in costume as O'Loughlin anyway—turns his attention to him.

"Yes?" he asks.

The steward looks at me and back at him. "There's no Mrs. Baker in B-49. In fact, the Bishops were quite confused as to why I would think the young lady is staying in their stateroom."

"What the hell?" I ask. The doctor and the steward both look at me with furrowed brows. "My mom, sister, and I are all staying in that room, B-49. Who the hell are the Bishops?"

The older woman gasps and covers her mouth. Great. So now we're pretending proper ladies don't swear. *Give me a freaking break.*

"Clearly, you're mistaken," the steward argues. "Perhaps you've forgotten your room number."

"I'm not—"

"The girl has had a head injury," Dr. O'Loughlin says quickly. "I'm sure this is all a misunderstanding." He looks at me the same way he did when I talked about my cell phone. "We'll find your family. Not to worry, dear."

"Worry about what?" It's such a relief to hear that deep, familiar voice. Sure, Will acted confused about what I was saying, too, but somehow I feel hopeful just having him in the room with me. But seconds later, a man and a woman step in behind him. They all look similar, with the same shaped eyes.

"Ah, Mr. Stewart, I'm glad you've returned," the doctor says. "It seems we have a misunderstanding."

"They're saying I have the room number wrong," I explain. "But I know for sure that's my room. I need to find my mom."

"Doctor," the steward says, and everyone turns to him. "I'm afraid it's more than that. I've also checked the manifest. There are no passengers named Isabelle Baker or anyone listed as Miss Allison Baker. They're simply not on the ship."

I crinkle my brow. "What?" *This is impossible.*

"I've checked and double checked," he insists.

The doctor shakes his head. "Dear, you've hit your head. Surely, it's possible that you're mistaken, isn't it?"

"I guess." He's looking at me the same way he would if a monkey just flew out my ass. I have to agree with him, or who knows what he might do. But I'm sure I'm right, and as soon as I get out of here, I'll find my family myself.

Will steps forward. "Regardless, we have a woman here who needs assistance finding her place," he says. "We must take action to assist her. She's most certainly confused after such a traumatic experience. I'll help her locate her family."

"Will—" The woman behind him frowns and glares at me like I'm an insect crawling on her toast.

He waves her off and continues speaking to the doctor. "The bandage on her head—is this something that needs to be changed regularly?"

Dr. O'Loughlin shakes his head. "No. She can take that off as soon as the bleeding stops. It's not a significant wound, and it didn't require any stitches."

"Then she's safe to leave your office and find her family herself, with my assistance of course?" he asks.

"Yes… at least, physically she's all right," Dr. O'Loughlin confirms. "Though I'm concerned with these misunderstandings—"

"There are no misunderstandings," I say firmly. "Yeah, I hit my head, but I'm fine. I'm one hundred percent positive that my family is staying in room B-49." I just don't understand how I could be wrong about that. We spent so much time before we left researching the room on the original *Titanic*.

A shocking realization hits me, and I feel the color draining from my face. The people who stayed in that room on the original *Titanic* were named Bishop…. What the fu–

"We'll sort this out, Millie," Will assures me. He turns back to the doctor. "I'll take responsibility for her. She can stay in my sister's room if need be."

"Will—" The woman, his sister, I guess, speaks up again, and she still doesn't look happy.

"I do suggest you get her a proper gown," the doctor says. He looks at me. "If you have any feelings of dizziness or imbalance, come back here immediately."

I nod. "Sure thing."

Will's sister and the other man pull him aside, and I can hear bits and pieces of their whispering argument. It's pretty clear that's what it is, especially by the look on his sister's face.

"No other place to go…."

"Not your responsibility, Will…."

I can't hear much more of their convo, but they don't seem particularly happy to help me out. They are right–I'm not Will's responsibility, but I would love to have his help. I sure the hell don't want to go parading around in this disgusting swimsuit any longer than I have to. Maybe his sister has some jeans and a T-shirt I can borrow.

Finally, Will turns around. "Don't worry," he tells me. "We'll get you something proper to wear, and you can stay in my sister's cabin, if we are unable to locate your mother." He looks at the doctor. "We'll take it from here."

"Good luck, dear," the doctor tells me.

It seems like I'm going to need it. I leave with them, and we head up a couple of flights of stairs and down a long hallway.

"This is my sister, Agatha." She nods but doesn't even turn to look at me as we continue on our way. "And this is my brother, Edward Stewart."

"Pleasure," Edward says, and I get the feeling he's happier to meet me than his sister.

"Nice to meet you both," I say.

We pass a few people along the way, and some of them give me a few stares. Of course, they're all wearing Edwardian clothes. *I don't know what's wrong with all these people.*

Finally, we reach what must be their rooms.

"Come inside quickly," Agatha says. "We need to get you into proper attire."

I look up at Will hopelessly as his sister nods toward the door. I'd much rather go into Will's room, but I guess I don't have a choice.

Maybe I am confused. *But how can that be?* With no other options, I go inside, and she closes the door behind us.

I hope I don't regret this.

5

WILL

I'M HESITANT TO LEAVE MILLIE ALONE WITH AGATHA, ESPECIALLY WITH the way my sister has been protesting lending our assistance to her in the first place. But there's nothing I can do as the door closes behind them.

"Come along," my brother says, shooing me into our room.

Safely inside away from prying ears in the hallway, I can open up. Edward has always been easier to talk to than Agatha. "I'm terribly concerned. Millie has been confused about more than simply the location of her family, but I didn't bring it up earlier. I was hoping she'd settle down after the doctor treated her."

"Oh?" He steps over to the cabinet to take down a couple of glasses and a bottle of brandy.

"She said odd things about the pool," I explain. "It seems she remembered it being on the top deck, outside."

"Outside?" He pours three fingers into each glass and hands me one. "That's preposterous. Who has ever heard of having a pool outside in the open? Anyone would be able to see the women in their bathing clothes."

"Exactly," I say. "And she went on about taking a photograph with a telephone."

He shakes his head, plopping down in the chair opposite me. "Well, obviously the hit on the head was a tad more dramatic than we realized. I'm sure the damage could have a great effect on one's thinking."

"I suppose," I agree, taking a sip. "But she seems so certain."

He nods. "She did seem rather confident when insisting she was right about the room number."

"You see what I mean?" I set my glass on the table. "It's troubling."

"The best thing to do is keep talking to her," he suggests. "Perhaps, over time, she'll start to see things as they are. It's likely a temporary malady. I'm sure it will pass."

"I hope so." We both look up to the sound of knocking on the connecting door between our room and Agatha's. "Come in."

I rise as Millie walks in, looking stunning in Agatha's light blue day dress, its color bringing out the crimson hues in her strawberry blonde hair. I hadn't even noticed the color when she was soaking wet. Though it's drier now and somewhat styled, she still wears the head bandage.

My sister walks in behind her. "I thought it best to forego the hat until the bandage is settled."

"The dress suits you," I say, wishing I could tell her how I really feel about it, though I'm not going to do that in front of my siblings. "Thank you, Agatha. I appreciate the help."

"It's nothing," she insists, but she still has that look on her face that says we should have nothing to do with Millie. I still can't help but want to assist her. She has no one else.

Edward sets his empty glass on the cabinet. "Agatha, let's go get a seat for lunch," he suggests. Looking at me, he adds, "Perhaps ring the steward to bring your meal to the stateroom. We ought not get everyone concerned about her injury." He nods toward Millie.

Her bandage is definitely not discreet. "Perhaps."

Agatha scoffs lightly. I'm sure she's reluctant to leave us alone in the room, but I'm certainly going to be a gentleman. I only want to ensure Millie is well. Thankfully, Edward scoots Agatha away, and we're left alone. It's not exactly proper, but under the circumstances, it is what it is.

"How are you feeling?" I ask.

She shrugs. "About the same, I guess. I haven't had any sharp pains since I first woke up, and the throbbing went away."

"No dizziness?"

"Nope," she replies—which I take to mean no. Her language is rather odd "I feel fine, and I can probably take this thing off." She unwinds her bandage before I decide whether it's proper to offer assistance. But it comes off easily, and her hair flows into place, framing her face with soft curls that make her face look even more elegant.

I clear my throat and divert my gaze. No reason to stare.

Thankfully, she's looking elsewhere, admiring the room. "It's amazing how authentic they made this. What deck are we on?"

"B Deck."

"So, your room is close to mine," she says. "It's strange we didn't run into each other before. At least, I don't remember seeing you. Did I?" I shrug, not sure what she's getting at. She runs her finger along the bureau. "Weird how this room doesn't seem as modernized as mine. I don't even see any charger outlets."

"I'm sorry?"

"You know, to charge your phone and stuff. There's no TV. either" She looks up at the calendar. "Oh, you even have a 1912 calendar. My room doesn't have that, either."

"I brought it to help me keep track of how long we're on the ship," I explain before taking a seat by the bookshelf and allowing her time to admire the stateroom. From what I'm aware, all the rooms on B Deck are quite similar, so she should be familiar with everything in mine. I still don't know what she means by "charging your phone." And what in the world is a TV?

Perhaps she's just gaining some memories. Maybe some questions will jog her memory.

"Where are you from, Millie?" I ask.

She spins around and comes over to sit in the adjacent chair. "Fishers, Indiana. It's a suburb of Indianapolis," she says. "Have you ever been there?"

I shake my head. "No, this is my first trip to America."

She cocks her head sideways. "What about New York City?"

"I've never been," I say, and she crinkles her forehead. "I'm looking forward to it, though."

She takes a little breath, her lips pursed together as though she's confused. "But we just left there."

I suppose she's still confused, so I ask another question. "What brought you to Southampton?"

"This boat, eventually," she says.

She's definitely not sorted her thoughts out yet. "I suppose news of the *RMS Titanic* could have reached Indianapolis," I say. "It's quite an impressive ship. That's a long way to travel just to turn around and go back for the maiden voyage, though."

"Turn around?"

"Yes, unless you spent some time enjoying my good country beforehand." She's still looking at me the same way.

"No, I've never been to England," she says. "We just left the port in New York...." She shakes her head. "Let's try something different. Where are you from?"

"Southampton," I explain, still confused but happy to change the subject. "I suppose that's what made me choose this ship for our voyage. That and all of the buzz about how luxurious it is. Agatha insisted." I chuckle.

"Hmm." She looks around the ship and back at me. "Most people are aboard for the nostalgia. My mom is a huge fan of the *RMS Titanic*."

It's strange that a woman would be so interested in ships. "Was her father a sailor?"

"What?" Her brow furrows again. "No. She just likes the history of the *Titanic*."

"Well, it's not much of a history at this point, is it? I suppose one could count its construction, which I understand took a few years." I have to admit, I admire the scope of the project.

"What are you talking about, Will? *Titanic* is over a hundred years old. Are we still doing this? Even in here, away from everyone else?"

I'm not sure how to respond, so I change the subject again. "I hope my sister was friendly with you."

She shakes her head and pulls at the collar of her dress like she's uncomfortable. "She was fine," she says. "I don't think she really wants to help me though. This dress is really pretty, but so freaking uncomfortable. How did they parade around in these gowns back then?" She pulls at the waistline. "God, they're so hard to wear. I wish she would've had some jeans, but when I asked her, she looked at me like I was insane. Are you guys planning to wear these authentic clothes the whole time?"

"Authentic?"

"Yes, for the period," she says. "It's amazing how her whole closet was filled with dresses like these, and while they all looked brand new, they all had a very strong vintage feel to them. They're not like costumes at all."

I frown, but I realize by the look in her eyes that she's not trying to insult Agatha. "Yes, my sister has a fine collection of gowns. The color of this one suits you."

Finally, she cracks a smile, and a touch of pink gives her cheeks a rosy glow. "Thank you. I guess everyone really wants to be authentic on this ship, but I would rather not wear the corset. I can barely breathe." She gives it another tug, but nothing changes.

Now it's my turn to blush. I certainly don't want to discuss women's undergarments with her. "Yes, well… I wouldn't know, obviously." I clear my throat. "You said your mother was fascinated by the ship. Where did she first hear about it? I'd imagine it takes some time for information to get from New York to Indiana. Does she often research new passenger liners?"

Millie's eyebrows nearly touch as she stares at me. "Uhm, no. Just this one. Mostly because of the movie."

"Movie?" Is she talking about a nickelodeon or something of that nature?

"Yes, Will. The movie!" Her eyes go wide as she turns toward me, like she is of the understanding that I should know precisely what she's speaking of.

I haven't the foggiest clue. "Which... which movie?"

"Come on! Sure, there've been dozens of movies about *Titanic*, but everyone knows the story of Jack and Rose." I stare at her blankly. She adds, "From the nineties?"

It still makes no sense to me. How could anyone make a nickelodeon about the *Titanic* in 1890 when the ship hadn't even been commissioned yet?

"She's made me watch it a bazillion times, especially before this trip." She rolls her eyes and takes a few steps, still looking around the room. "It wasn't terrible. Anyway, after that she really got into it. She read every book she could find about it and made us sit through enough documentaries that every detail is all up here." She points to her head.

"I'm sorry... documentaries?" Some of the phrases she uses are confusing.

"Yes, you know, like on the History Channel or whatever, those long shows about true things," she explains.

"How do you come to watch so many picture shows?" I ask.

"Picture shows?" she giggles. "I suppose you could call them that. I mean, I have hundreds of streaming channels."

I shake my head. "I apologize. I don't understand what that means."

She giggles again, and I love the musical ring to it, but I'm still confused. "I think you're taking this cosplay thing a bit too far. I get it. You're keeping up the act like it's 1912."

I have no idea what a cosplay is, but I decide not to ask. "Well, that's because it is."

"Okay, you stay in 1912, but I'd rather be in real time in 2025."

My brows raise, and I stare at her for a moment, waiting for her to say she's only carrying on. But she doesn't. And then, a sudden real-ization hits me. "You think we're in 2025?" Her blue eyes don't waiver from mine as she stares back at me. "Millie, I assure you, the year is most definitely 1912."

She holds my gaze a few more moments before she rolls her eyes. "Yeah, we're supposed to pretend that it's 1912 or whatever, but I'm over it," she says. "I think you're really convincing, and that's great. Are you practicing to be an actor one day or something? If that's the case, you don't have to keep it up around me. It's honestly starting to get super annoying."

I sink down on the edge of the couch and drag my hands down my face. I've never heard of a condition like this, but it seems quite clear she does, in fact, think that she's from the future. All of these odd contraptions she's speaking of, her strange way of speaking, it must be part of the story her mind has constructed after her injury that has her concluding she's from another time.

I shake my head. "No, honestly, Millie, it is 1912. Perhaps that bump on the head was more severe than the doctor realized."

"Okay, Will," she says in a strange, childlike voice, making a face at me. "It's 1912. Whatever you say. God, give it up already. I appreciate your help, but it's getting old, my friend."

I want to tell her again that it's not an act, but if she has an injury so severe she thinks she's from 2025, perhaps it's best to let her think what she wants until she comes to realize the truth on her own.

I suppose it's good she considers me to be a friend. I would like to help her—if I can.

"So, would you like to request lunch, or should we go look for your mother and sister?" I ask instead.

She smiles, and it lights up her eyes. "I'm hungry, but I'd absolutely like to find my family first. God, they're gotta be so worried about me."

"Yes, I suppose they must be." I give her a reassuring smile and escort her out the door, my eyes on her quizzically as she walks down the hallway. Something is quite strange about this woman, and yet... I find her captivating.

6

My head is spinning from that conversation. I don't know why he's so determined to keep up this act, but maybe he's a paid actor or something. Is it possible that only some of us are actual passengers, and maybe the rest are all actors who need to play their roles to make it more authentic? It's strange that he stayed in character in private, though.

Looking around, something seems off. "We're on B Deck?" I ask.

Will nods. "Correct. Your stateroom should be right down this way."

Things only look vaguely familiar, but he's right. My room should be close by if we're really on B Deck. "Yes, but where are all the old photos?"

"I'm afraid I have never seen any portraits in the corridor," he says.

"Well, the hallway where my room is looks a lot like this with all this white paneling, but there were historical pictures of the ship hung all along here." I frown, looking up and down the hall and seeing none. "This is really weird. Why would they take them down?"

He exhales but says nothing, looking at me with a furrowed brow. I guess we're going around in circles again. This just doesn't make any sense.

We reach B-49. "Now, I know there was a photo of the launch here. I look at it every time I come back to the room."

"You seem so certain that you aren't in 1912," he says. "I assure you, that's precisely the year."

"*Sure*, it's 1912." I shake my head. This is starting to get old. "Let's just find my mom."

"Very well." He knocks on the door, and a man with a long beard answers. He's wearing an old-fashioned suit, a perfect costume right down to the sparkling pocket watch chain.

I don't get it. *Why would Mom invite this man to our room?*

"I'm terribly sorry to interrupt you," Will says. "May I ask if this happens to be Mrs. Baker's room?"

The man frowns and shakes his head. "You're the second lad to come asking about this Baker woman. I'm afraid there is no one in this room by that name. I'm Mr. Dickenson Bishop, and my wife is the only woman residing here at the moment. I'm afraid there's been a mistake."

"What the hell?" I shout. "This is definitely my room, Will." The man looks at me like he can't believe I'm even talking.

Will holds up a hand and gives Mr. Bishop a polite smile. I push up on my tiptoes to look over his shoulder. I don't see my mom or sister, and the room looks different. There's nothing but a fancy dresser where the TV should be.

"I assure you, miss, my wife and I have been in this stateroom since we boarded," the man says. "Now, if you'll pardon me…."

"We're terribly sorry to disturb you, sir," Will tells him. He takes me by the arm and leads me away.

"But that's my room," I complain, walking backward as he pulls me gently down the hallway. "My mom and Ally should be in there. Actually, they should be with me. Why would they leave me when I hit my head and fell in the pool?" There's so much that isn't right about all this.

"I am just as confused as you are," he insists. "But we aren't likely to find a solution in that stateroom with the Bishop family."

"I'm positive that's my room—B-49." I turn around, watching a couple pass us in the hallway. They also look like they belong in 1912. They avert their eyes as if avoiding us—me anyway. Once they pass, I run my finger beneath my collar. The lace is scratchy, and it's so tight I feel like I can hardly breathe.

I'd love to get out of this elaborate dress, but I don't have anything else to wear. I guess it was nice of his sister to help me put it on, which I probably couldn't have done on my own. It's pretty, I'll admit, but it came with so many layers, I could be out on an Arctic exposition and probably not get cold. Agatha's eyes nearly bulged out of her head when I asked if she had any jeans I could wear. All this pretending like it's 1912 is going way too far.

"Why don't we take a moment to lounge on the promenade?" Will suggests. "The fresh air will do you good, and we can discuss why the situation is so confusing at the moment."

I nod. Sounds good." We head toward the upper deck, but still, all of the historical photos are missing from the walls. I don't even see any empty nails or holes in the paint where they used to be. The whole ship was full of them so we could all see what things looked like back in the day. But now, there's nothing.

We step on the deck, and even the scent is different. Now, the sea water smell is mixed with something that's definitely not diesel fuel. I take a deep whiff, and it reminds me of the time I went to see an authentic train with my mom. Could that be… coal?

Everywhere I look, I see people dressed like it's really 1912. I don't see the bikini girls anywhere.

"My brother rented some deck chairs over this way," he says, leading me to the left.

"Why did they need to rent them?" I ask. "There were plenty of lounge chairs on the deck." But as soon as I say it, I notice they're all gone. A few people are sitting in wooden chairs that don't look very comfortable, and there are also several benches attached to the deck.

"We had to rent them for the voyage," he explains. "Perhaps your mother rented yours and didn't explain that to you."

"No." I shake my head. I'm about to say something else but notice another difference. "Where are all the lifeboats?"

"Those are scattered throughout the promenade," he explains. "See, there are several over there."

I turn to look where he's pointing and notice the cluster of lifeboats looks more like what I saw in that movie Will's allegedly never heard of. I know that *Titanic 2* is bigger than the original ship for several reasons, but also so that we have enough lifeboats for everyone—a law that was changed because of the sinking of the original ship. "Where are the other ones that were hanging over there?" I'm pretty sure this is our muster station. Our boats are gone.

Will doesn't answer me. Instead, he gestures at some chairs, and we both sit. This one is not nearly as comfortable as the one I sat in earlier today—before the bathing suit fiasco. "Perhaps we should try another way. You come from 2025, you say?" I nod.." Tell me about life there. I'm sure there are many changes. What sort of inventions or discoveries might I find interesting?"

"Oh, okay. We're still doing this then." I sigh as his forehead furrows. He's going to win an Oscar one day. " Well, uhm, there are a lot of things, but for starters, people usually fly when they want to go someplace too far to drive. Cruise ships are just for fun when you want something different for vacation."

Will tips his head to the side. "Did you say... fly? Surely, in 2025, people haven't sprouted wings."

I laugh. "No, of course not. I mean on airliners. Jets." He's still staring at me, so I continue. "Okay then. I guess we're pretending like you don't know what that is. You've heard of the Wright Brothers?"

"Of course, but there's no way more than one or two people could ever fit on an aeroplane."

"Hundreds of people fly on one plane at the same time." I see the shock register in his eyes. "Also, we have cell phones, and I feel lost without mine. It's always in my pocket."

"How could one fit an entire telephone in a pocket? Where are the wires?"

"They're wireless," I explain. "They look something like—" I look around, and nobody has one, but one man is reading a book not far from us. "They're shaped something like a very small, thin book."

There's that shock in his eyes again. Seriously? This guy should definitely win an Academy Award for Best Actor.

"I guess computers are the next thing," I add. "Pretty much everyone has a laptop. Well, our phones are minicomputers these days since we can search the Internet on smartphones, but we also have desktops or laptops for doing that."

"The... Internet?" Will repeats, saying it slowly, like he could potentially figure out what it might be if he dissects the parts.

"Yeah, God. I don't even know how to explain that. You're really putting me through the wringer. Um, I don't know all the technical details, but you go to websites and find information or just watch cat videos if that's what you want. It's pretty much anything you want to know, you search for it, and it's right there."

"This is all terribly difficult to imagine." He runs a hand through his hair, making it stand up a bit before the wind settles it back down. "I'm afraid I don't understand many of these strange words. What is a website? I assume it has nothing to do with spiders."

"Are you seriously going to make me explain what a website is?"

His eyes widen slightly. "If you'd rather not, I understand. It's just... I can't imagine what you're referring to."

"Okay, fine. We'll do it your way." I take a deep breath and consider how to explain what a website is. "So... it's kind of like a movie–a nickelodeon? You know what that is?

He nods, still looking confused.

"Right, so there are millions of them. They each have an address. You type it in, and you go to the website, and it shows you pictures or you can read information. It used to be a lot of shit for school, like history junk. But now, there's a lot of entertainment. There are sites for sharing videos and stuff like that."

I can tell by his expression that he isn't following. It seems...

impossible. But he genuinely looks confused. He shakes his head. "I'm afraid I'm unable to imagine what that might look like."

A nervous laugh bubbles out of my mouth. I've seen some really good acting before, but in the back of my mind, I'm starting to wonder... could he seriously not know what I'm talking about. "You weren't born in a barn by any chance, were you?"

"A barn?"

"Never mind." I twirl a long lock of hair around my finger and stare out at the ocean. Maybe when we get to Southampton, I'll know for sure what's happening. It might be easy to change the decade on an isolated ship than in an entire city.

"I wish there was something I could do to convince you," Will says, taking a deep breath. I really do want to believe him. The man saved my life–why would he be lying to me. "I have an idea."

Will stands up and walks to the railing, and I follow. ""What are we looking at?"

"Look there." He points up at the sun. "Do you know the time?"

"Uhm, well, it should be about four in the afternoon," I surmise, based on when we went out to the pool and how much time seems to have passed.

He pulls out a pocket watch, checks it, and nods. "That's right. Look where the sun is. If we were sailing to Southampton, we would be going east, but you can tell by the position of the sun that we are, in fact, sailing west. We're headed to New York City, Millie."

My heart thumps in my chest as I try to process his words. He's right. I'm no scientist, but I know the sun sets in the west. "Shit," I murmur. My legs start to feel weak. I stumble back to the chairs and sit down, and Will joins me.

"Are you well, Millie?" I can hear the concern in his voice. He places a hand gently on my arm, and it's oddly comforting, despite my discomfort.

I stare into his eyes and realize he doesn't know what I'm talking about because he's never seen any of it before. "Will, this can't be happening. I really don't know how the hell is going on, but I'm scared. Either I'm dreaming, hallucinating, or I'm really in 1912... on

42

the *RMS Titanic*." I think of my mom and sister. God, they must be so scared. Do they know where I'm at?

"Millie, I truly do not know what to make of all this," he says. "I apologize, but your story just sounds so fantastic. I don't know how it can be true. I truly want to believe you."

"I guess I can't blame you for that," I admit, another nervous giggle escaping my lips. "It does sound crazy." I look around as panic fills my veins. These are real passengers on the *Titanic*, and I'm one of them now.

Oh, my God. Somehow, I'm really here. And how I got here really doesn't matter anymore because, unlike all these people, I know what's going to happen.

Visions from that movie fill my mind. The iceberg. The bits of ice on the deck. The laughing and carrying on, everyone thinking they're perfectly safe. And then... the horror when the boat starts to go down.

I turn and look him in the eyes, and even though I'm going to be lying the crazy on even thicker, I know I have to tell him what I know. "Will, I'm going to tell you something else, and you need to believe me."

"I want to believe you, Millie," he says, his warm hand still on my arm. "I do honestly believe that you think you're from the future."

I turn toward him and place both of my hands on his upper arms. "Yes, that's because I am from the future. Listen, there's something else. Something really, really bad."

He sits up straight and leans in. "Millie, I understand how frightened you are. I can't blame you. Hopefully, this delusion will wear off soon, and we'll get it all sorted out. You'll be perfectly fine."

I shake my head vigorously. "You don't understand. I won't be. None of us will be."

"I understand it appears that way now," he insists. "Once we arrive in New York City, I'll ensure that you are safe and provided for until we find your family."

"That's what I'm trying to tell you, Will!" Panic and exasperation surge through me as I stare into his calm blue eyes. "We're not going to make it to New York City!"

"What's that now?" His forehead crinkles, and he shakes his head. Now, he's the one laughing. "I assure you, we will," he says. "This ship is unsinkable, or so they say. My family will help you–"

"It's not as unsinkable as you think," I say, shaking my head.

"Of course we will." He's still scoffing at me, but I hear a hint of concern I hadn't before.

I lean in, looking around at the others near us before I whisper, "I'm telling you, we won't get to New York. Will, this ship is going to sink."

7

"SINK?" I'M CAREFUL TO REPEAT THE WORD QUIETLY SO AS NOT TO alarm the nearby passengers, no matter how preposterous the idea. I wouldn't want anyone to panic or begin to listen in on what they would naturally find to be an absurd conversation..

"Yes, sink," she insists, thankfully still whispering. "Everyone said it was unsinkable until it hit an iceberg and sank."

I sit back in the deck chair, struggling to decide what to make of it. She sounds like a madwoman, yet she is so certain about everything she's saying. But I didn't choose the ship for our voyage lightly. "In Southampton, the press followed its construction closely, as did my brother and I. They offered quite some detail about its design. There are several safeguards to ensure that sinking is quite impossible."

"You don't get it," she insists. "That's what everyone thought. But everyone was wrong. That's why there aren't enough lifeboats."

I look around. The number of lifeboats on the deck does seem scant for the number of people aboard, but then, that's not unusual.

"If it didn't sink, this ship probably wouldn't have been such a big

45

deal," she adds. "And there wouldn't be so many movies, books, and websites about it."

"Websites? The things that are like books—but on some sort of contraption." I still can't fully picture what she means by that.

"Exactly."

"Your head injury may have you confused," I suggest, trying to be gentle. Whatever the case, she's clearly upset. "Perhaps you had a dream about a shipwreck that's now mingling with your thoughts because of the blow to your skull. Or you may have read a story about such an event. But I assure you, you are safe aboard the *Titanic*. This is the largest ship in the world. She's built solid. The hull has compartments that are watertight. It cannot sink."

"Tell that to Jack and Rose."

"Come again?"

"Never mind. Yes, it had sixteen supposedly watertight compartments." I raise a brow, surprised she knows the details. "When it hit the iceberg, it ripped into the ship, plus they had weak rivets that pulled the compartments apart even more. It's not watertight if it can rip."

"The construction was not up to par?" I ask.

"Not in that case," she confirms.

"How do you know so much about the ship?" It's so unusual for a woman to be so knowledgeable about such things.

"The History Channel is pretty thorough."

"Now I'm confused." I shake my head. "Of which ocean channel are you referring?"

"It's not an ocean. It's a channel on TV," she says, but I still have no idea what she means.

"TV?"

She lets out an exasperated sigh. "Never mind that. You—*we* are still a few decades before TVs. The important thing is that the water spilled over the bulkheads, and eventually, the ship started to sink. It even broke in half as it went down."

I shake my head again, looking around at the huge, sturdy ship beneath our feet. Compared to smaller liners I've been on, the ride is smooth, so much so that it's difficult to tell we're at sea.

"It was an iceberg?"

"Yes."

Inhaling, I try to imagine that possibility.

Her green eyes lock with mine. "You still don't believe me."

"I want to." I gaze at the setting sun. Its position was effective in convincing her she really was here sailing toward America. Perhaps there is a way I can understand her perspective through similar means. "Very well," I say, sitting up and facing her. "Tell me all the details you know about the *Titanic*."

Her eyes look hopeful. "That's way too much info, and we probably don't have time, but okay. Um, I already explained the iceberg and the bulkheads. What else? Oh... the people! I remember a lot of names. The Astors... um, John Jacob the Fourth—he's the richest person on board, a real estate developer. His second wife was—is only eighteen and pregnant, and she came with him on the *Titanic*."

I'm surprised she's so blunt about the woman's condition. I look around to ensure no one can hear, but the other passengers seem to be oblivious to our conversation.

"They were going back to America to have the baby," she continues. "There's Margaret Brown. After she survives, they call her the unsinkable Molly Brown. She's quite a character, that one. Um, Isidor and Ida Straus; they owned Macy's. That store gets huge, by the way. They have a parade every Thanksgiving with giant character balloons. Mr. Ismay from White Star Lines—I forget his first name—and Thomas Andrews, who designed the ship, were both on board because it's the maiden voyage. I guess they wanted to see how it would go, which was, yeah, not very well."

"I'm familiar with Mr. Ismay and Mr. Andrews, but not all of the others," I admit. A lot of them are American, and I don't keep up with socialites from overseas.

"They're pretty much famous," she adds. "Oh, there were so many names. It's hard to remember them all now. I do remember a few third-class passengers who survived," she adds. "A couple of names stick in my head for some reason—Mary Elizabeth Davidson and Catherine Connolly. And then there's Millvina."

"I don't know any third-class passengers," I tell her with a shrug.

"Well, yeah, you totally wouldn't because they separated people," she says. "I can't believe they treated people like that. God, especially during the sinking."

I can't say I approve of separating people by class, either. Even some of the first-class passengers have refused our dinner invitations, thinking themselves above us. Everyone clamors to dine with the Astors.

"I'm named after Millvina," she explains. "She's the youngest survivor, and was only nine weeks old…. Well, I guess she *is* only nine weeks old. To think she's down there now…." Her eyes start to sparkle with moisture as she looks down and puts a curved finger over her mouth thoughtfully.

The thought of a child in danger moves me as well, and her story feels so genuine. I find myself wanting to alleviate her sadness, so I try to pivot the conversation. "So, Millie is short for Millvina?" I ask softly.

She looks up, and I see both sadness and fear in her eyes. "No, it's Millicent." She takes a breath. "Mom sort of named me after her, but she thought Millicent was slightly less cringe."

I have no idea what she means by that, but I decide not to ask.

"Um, I also know about lots of crew members." She brushes away a strand of her strawberry blonde hair. "Four officers make it. Charles Lightoller was Second Officer. I think Herbert Pitman was Third Officer. The others were Joseph Boxhall and Harold Lowe. I forget their ranks." She lowers her voice again. "No other officers of the ship survive the disaster."

I nod gravely, though I'm unfamiliar with the names of the crew. It does seem she knows several details. Either her imagination is quite elaborate, or these people are real.

I actually think I'm starting to believe her.

"I also know about the two wireless operators who sent out the distress calls." Her eyes shift up as if to recall, then come back to mine.

"Harold Bride and Jack Phillips were—are their names. They brought the *RMS Carpathia* here. That was the closest ship that responded, but even that was hours away. It took too long to save anyone. It was all up to the lifeboats. Will, we're on our own out here."

I don't have a clue whether those names are correct or not, but I have to admit, she's quite convincing.

"And I don't even know how I got here, but I'm not supposed to be here," she adds, her growing concern obvious. "Who knows if I'm going to make it or not?" Her next words are whispered. "This is bad, very bad. I could die here. We could both die here."

"I'm not going to let that happen." My words are swifter than I intend, but I feel them intensely. Many of her claims do ring true. Perhaps the bulkheads are not as impenetrable as the ship's designers intended. "I'm starting to believe you, Millie. If everything will happen as you say, I promise I'll make every effort to protect you."

I see a tear form in her left eye as her countenance shifts to melancholy. "Thanks. I don't blame you for thinking I'm crazy. This is all nuts, and I barely believe it myself. But how will we—" She shakes her head, puts both hands on her face, and begins to cry.

Patting her shoulder just doesn't seem sufficient to console a woman who thinks she may die. I move my deck chair closer to hers and pull her into my arms.

Her effect feels different to me now that I'm holding her. The strength that defied Mr. Bishop and the doctor has melted away, and now she seems so small and timid, vulnerable. I hold her close as her quiet sobbing continues, well aware of the eyes around us turning inquisitively in our direction. I'm not concerned about the unwanted attention.

The same urge to protect her I felt when I saw her thrashing around in the pool has returned. "We're going to figure this out," I try to assure her as I offer my handkerchief.

She nods, yet her sobbing continues as she wraps her warm hand around my forearm and moves in closer. So many thoughts race through my mind. I don't know the passenger count, but it's at least two thousand souls. In my visage, there are only two lifeboats, spread quite a way apart. I can't see any others, though I know there are more. Not a lot more, however. Surely there aren't enough to rescue everyone should the ship go down.

Unease settles in my nerves as I realize I'm considering the possibility that *Titanic* will sink. *Am I becoming entangled in Millie's lunacy?*

Finally, her sobbing begins to ease, and we part, leaning back into our own chairs. "I'm sorry," she says.

"Nonsense," I tell her. "It's quite all right. You're upset, and you have every right to be."

"Unless I'm insane."

I shake my head. "You believe you're in danger, and I truly am beginning to believe you. With what you've told me, grown men would cry under such circumstances. You're being quite brave."

"I guess."

My mind fills with flashes of Millie sinking helplessly in the pool. How strange that none of the men nearby had seen her before she fell. There were at least a dozen, I among them, and I didn't see her fall in or notice her anywhere in the room beforehand. That wouldn't be possible in a men's-only swim.

It was as if she appeared from nowhere.

Could she have truly fallen in from the future?

8

MILLIE

I DIDN'T MEAN TO CRY IN FRONT OF ALL THESE PEOPLE, AND I'M A little embarrassed but mostly just plain exhausted. This is way too much to think about.

"I think I'd like to go back to the room and rest." I stand and stare at the handkerchief in my hand, now wet with tears and probably some snot. *Do I offer it back to him?* It's not like I've ever been around a guy who keeps a handkerchief in his pocket before.

He seems to catch on. "You can keep it. I have several."

Thank God. I crumble it up in my hand and reach down for a pocket. Of course, there aren't any, despite the forty layers of cloth this contraption of a dress has. How were women supposed to carry anything? I guess it's a good thing I don't have my cell phone with no pockets. And the men probably had all the money and the keys to everything. I bet Will has plenty of pockets.

"I'll escort you back to the room," he says.

It finally makes sense why he's been so convincing—because he's exactly who he said he is. He holds out his elbow, and I slip my arm through. I kind of like that, actually. Most of the guys I've dated would just start walking and expect me to follow. No, they wouldn't even walk me back to the room. It'd just be, "See ya!"

That might've been enough to make me laugh if I weren't in the middle of one of the worst disasters ever. *Shit, what am I going to do?*

"I can see your point about the lifeboats," he says. "They hardly seem sufficient."

I shake my head. "They aren't. If the deck was filled with lifeboats, who would have believed the ship was unsinkable? Plus, it wouldn't look nice. It's all about the luxury. They had to sell it. Not to mention the standards were different back then–now."

"Do you honestly think that's what it is?" Will asks me. "Selling tickets over safety?"

I'm quiet for a moment as a couple passes. "Well, that and because it wasn't required. Why spend extra money when it messes up your whole 'luxury liner' vibe?"

He exhales, looking like he's thinking about my explanation. I'm still not sure he believes me, even though he said he did twice. I can't think of anything else that would convince him I'm telling the truth, short of the ship hitting the actual iceberg, and I'd rather have a plan before that happens.

We get to B Deck, and now it makes sense why there aren't any historical pictures. It's not history yet. *God, this is a mess.*

He unlocks his sister's door and leads me in. No one's here, but I hear voices next door. "Sounds like they're both in my room. Try to rest, and I'll meet you at dinner."

"Okay." I sit on the bed in my uncomfortable dress and start slipping off the shoes pinching my feet. As he turns the knob to the adjoining room, I speak up. "Will?"

"Yes?"

"Thank you for believing me." I give him a little smile. I don't know why he's even stuck with me this long with all the crazy things I've said.

"Of course," he says. "Please get some rest. We'll talk more later."

I nod as he leaves, pulling off the shoes. They're more like boots, but they have such pointy toes, I don't see how anyone can stand them. I guess that's just what's available now, and they're probably a lot easier to walk in than stilettos. I guess fashion will always be uncomfortable.

How I'm going to relax in this dress, I have no idea, but I know from getting into it that I'll never be able to get out of it by myself, and Agatha seems more than busy next door.

"Dinner? You're spending too much time with this woman as it is," I hear her say. *Great. She hates me already.* I can imagine how she'll feel when he tells her I'm a crazy woman who thinks she's from the future.

"We can't very well leave her in the room for dinner," Will argues.

They seem to realize I can hear them because their next words are murmurs. I lie back, resigned to being stuck in my prison of a dress while I try to close my eyes and rest. The neckline is so scratchy and uncomfortable.

I wonder how I got here. There's no such thing as time travel, right? Even if there was, it would be something people would do on purpose, like going back to play the lotto after knowing the jackpot numbers. All I did was hit my head on a swimming pool..

Wait—I'm here, and I know what's going to happen. Does that mean I can change history? I could tell everyone we're going to hit an iceberg and when it will happen. Maybe they'll slow down the ship and not hit the iceberg in the first place. Or they might turn in time, if they don't go hard to starboard, which is what made them turn slower.

Right. They're going to listen to some crazy woman who thinks she's from the future. They don't even listen to women in 1912. We don't get the luxury of dresses with pockets!

Almost two thousand people die on this ship. Maybe saving them is the wrong thing to do anyway. Every person is connected to so many other people, the ripple effects through time could change everything. Not to mention some good did come out of this disaster—like requiring a certain number of lifeboats. The weight of having to determine whether or not to try to stop this ship from going down is way too much for me to handle at the moment.

I hear Will in the other room. They're speaking louder again, still arguing. "Do this for me, Agatha."

"All right, I'll get her another of my gowns," I hear his sister say. "I just hope she doesn't make a fuss like she did before."

Yep, she hates me. I pull the pillow over my head trying to drown out the conversation, which thankfully quiets down again. My own family is probably panicked right now. Do they think I'm dead? I didn't actually die–did I? Or maybe I'm in a coma or I physically disappeared from that time just like I reappeared here.

Maybe there's no way for me to go back.

Mom, are you looking for me?

* * *

My eyes open, and I face a familiar wall. It's the *Titanic*, but is it the real one or the copy in my time? I can't tell the direction I'm facing.

"God, I hope this was all a dream."

I hear the doorknob turn and open, the one leading to the adjoining cabin. I really don't remember whether the room in my time had a door to the next room over or not.

"I see you're up."

It's Agatha's voice. *Oh, God.* It wasn't a dream. I'm on the real *Titanic*!

"I've waited as long as I could, but I'm afraid we must get dressed for dinner," she says.

I sit up and put my hand to my head. "Dressed? We're already dressed."

She looks at me like I'm crazy. "Goodness, you really have hit your head hard. You're wearing a day dress. We need to put on formal gowns for dinner."

Nodding, I stand, gazing at the shoes I took off and hoping I don't have to wear them again. I'd give anything for my worn-out Nikes.

But for now, I turn around and let her unfasten the back of this itchy-collared dress, feeling like I can breathe fresh air as soon as she loosens it. She helps me out of the layers, but then I watch as she lays out even more for the new dress.

I slide the chemise on first. "This is nice. Silk?"

"Yes, thank you," she says. "I prefer that to cotton for evenings."

"I see what you mean." I look helplessly at the pile of material on the bed.

"The corset is next." Her tone is calm and patient, surprisingly. Maybe Will told her I lost my memory.

But I hate corsets, and I see what Mom was talking about when she told me how lucky I am to live in the twenty-first century as Agatha pulls on the strings. "Can you make it just a little looser?"

Despite the exasperated sigh behind me, I feel it relax slightly. It still won't be easy to sit and eat.

"The drawers are next."

These look like clown pants, gathered at the waist and each leg. Gazing in the mirror, I see it looks like my waist is extra small, and I have big, rounded hips. I chuckle a bit. "Early twentieth century Photoshop."

"I'm sorry?"

"Nothing." I know the petticoat is next, so I put it on. I have no idea what dress I'm wearing until she pulls it out of the closet. I can't help but gasp when I see it.

"It's gorgeous." I'm so relieved that it has a square neckline, so at least my neck won't be itchy. The top of the blouse is sewn in an art deco style, which is very modern for Agatha. I'm sort of surprised. A jacket of the same silky material goes over it, and it takes Agatha quite a while to adjust the sash and fasten a large cameo brooch to the center.

"There we are," she says. "It's one of my favorites, but I don't wish to wear it twice in one week."

She hands me another pair of boot-like shoes, and I cringe, but they're just slightly wider in the toes than the other ones. They're stiff, but I can make them work. She has me sit on the vanity bench while she twists my hair into an updo, fastens it with large gold hair-pins, and attaches a large clip with flowers on it that matches my dress.

"You're ready," she announces finally. It's her turn to do the same routine, and I help her fasten things in the back and lace up the corset.

"I can't tell you how difficult it's been without a servant," she says. "I had to ask some of the other ladies to send me a maid to do this."

"I'm happy to help." I wonder why she doesn't have a maid when she's in first class, but I decide not to ask.

She does her hair in much the same way and looks very nice in her burgundy dress, which goes well with her blonde hair. I hope she likes me better for helping her.

"Let's go tell my brothers we're ready."

I nod and take a deep breath, wondering what Will will think of me in this dress. I follow her out to the main living area, and Agatha knocks on the common door first then opens it. We step in together. Will is facing the other way, straightening his collar in the mirror.

When he turns and sees me, his mouth drops open.

9

WILL

IT'S DIFFICULT TO FIND THE RIGHT WORDS FOR A MOMENT AS I TAKE IN Millie's beauty. She looks stunning in the green evening gown my sister has given her to wear. Though it certainly hasn't escaped me that she's quite lovely, I wasn't prepared for this.

"Will, you look very nice," she says.

I realize now that too much awkward silence has passed when I should have been complimenting her, yet I don't want to truly speak my mind. "Your hair goes with the dress." Certainly not what I intended to say. "You look lovely, Millie."

She chuckles a bit and flashes a smile as a hint of blush tinges her cheeks, which surprisingly gives me a light flutter in my heart. "Thanks."

Edward's voice rings out behind me. "Mm, shall we get to dinner, then?"

Grateful for the opportunity to leave the awkward moment behind, I offer Millie my arm. "If you're ready."

"I'm starving." She wraps her hand around my arm while Agatha gives her usual grunt of disapproval, and we escort the ladies to the dining hall.

"I hear they're offering the duck," Edward says to Agatha as they walk behind us.

"Excellent," she says. "I do enjoy a good duck."

Millie makes a face that clearly shows she's not pleased. I wonder if perhaps she doesn't like duck, but then she smiles as she looks up at me for a moment before gazing ahead.

"You seem in better spirits," I tell her. "The rest must have done you good."

She nods and keeps up the smile, but I can see the worry still alive in her eyes. "Yeah, I'm still scared, but I've gotta eat."

"Indeed." A member of the dining staff opens the door as we approach, and I nod as we pass him. "We'll need another place setting at our table."

"Of course," he says, hurrying to secure a chair and alert the kitchen staff to set out the dinnerware. I lead Millie over to our table, situated between two Corinthian columns near the center of the dining room. The gentlemen of our usual group rise to greet us.

"Will, my boy," Mr. Brandeis says, "I see we have a new guest at our table."

"We do." I stand back a bit while the servers set Millie's place. "May I present Miss Millicent Baker, a dear friend of Agatha's from boarding school."

Millie looks at me quizzically for a moment, but I continue with the introductions. "Miss Baker, this is Mr. Brandeis, Mr. and Mrs. Hippach, and Miss Allen."

"Pleasure," Mr. Brandeis says, and the others respond in kind.

"Good to meet you," Millie says, a bit more formally than her usual speech. I can't hold back a small smile of amusement as I pull out her chair.

I nod at the waiter as he hands me the menu. "I already know I'll have the salmon," I tell him before turning to Millie. "Would you prefer the fish, chicken, lamb, or duck?"

She inhales lightly. "Um, I'll go with the fish."

"Lamb for me," Edward says. "And my sister will have the duck."

Mr. Hippach speaks up when the server leaves. "None of you have spoken of Miss Baker before. Were you aware she was on board?"

"We were not." I shake my head. "We became reacquainted only recently. It's quite a coincidence."

Agatha manages a smile and a nod, but I can tell this is taxing her patience.

"I see," he says. "Well, what a lucky accident."

Millie hitches a breath at the word. I also see the hint of pink rising in her cheeks, and she fiddles with her skirt below the table. I suppose I should have told her ahead of time the story Edward and I had devised to explain her presence.

"Indeed," I say.

"Miss Baker, I'd love for you to join us for tea tomorrow afternoon," Mrs. Hippach says.

"That would be nice, thank you." I'm impressed with how well Millie is playing the role.

"We were just discussing the excitement in the pool," Mr. Brandeis says.

I can feel Millie stiffen beside me.

Mrs. Hippach nods. "I think it's just horrible. What kind of a woman sneaks into the men's swimming session and jumps into the pool?"

"She must be some kind of lunatic," Miss Allen agrees.

"Or she was sneaking in to get a look at the men swimming." Mr. Hippach chuckles.

"Scandalous," his wife adds with a huff.

"I'm sure the crew has it all handled." Edward nods as the server brings his drink. "I'm sure it was just a single incident."

"I should hope so," Miss Allen says.

"I have every confidence it was," Agatha chimes in. I see her pat Millie on the arm reassuringly. My sister has her doubts about Millie, but she would never sell her out in public. Millie seems to relax after that, copying the way Agatha handles her napkin. I wonder for a moment about the eating habits in 2025. *Are things so different in the future?*

Thankfully, the soup arrives, and our companions move to more intimate conversations among themselves.

"You're doing well," I whisper to Millie. "I apologize for the surprise about boarding school."

"No, that's fine," she insists. "It's a good idea. How else would you guys have met me?"

I let out a light chuckle. Her way of speaking is so charming in its own way.

She looks around the dining room. "It's hard to recognize anyone from old black and white photos of them. Can you point out a few people?"

I nod, finishing my spoonful of soup. "Over there in the large corner table, that's Mr. Astor, the one you spoke of."

"I should have known by his young wife, and how everyone is kissing up."

I laugh at her blunt, and correct, assessment of the situation.

"He won't survive," she whispers, and I find it startles me to the core. "She will. She'll live, but she'll lose her fortune when she remarries. She chooses her childhood friend over the trust fund JJ left her. Their son ends up with some money, but not all of it. He marries and has children. Dies in the nineties, I think."

"That's quite a lot of detail," I murmur.

She shrugs. "He was one of the most famous people."

It certainly makes sense, given his fortune.

"That must be Margaret Brown at the table next to his," she says. "I can tell by the way she's handling herself."

"I haven't made her acquaintance, but you may be right."

"I know I am." She gives me a crooked smile. "She survives, as I told you. Her husband made a fortune in mining. But he didn't like being a social butterfly."

Such a strange term, though I can deduce its meaning.

"They separated, but she still wanted to be a famous socialite," she adds. "She's a nice lady. She helped other people get into lifeboats before they made her get in herself, and she even helped row. She wanted to come back and save people, but it was too late."

I look over at the woman. She's laughing and slapping her thigh beneath the table. It's almost as if she doesn't fit in either, but if what Millie said about her character is true, It's easy to admire that.

"She fought for women's rights after that, which is definitely needed," she continues. "One day, women will be ordering food for themselves"

I wonder if I was rude not to hand her my menu, but it would have been admittedly awkward.

"No worries." She seems to sense my concern. "It's just the time you were born in."

I nod. There's so much more I want to know about Millie and her time, if everything she says is true. The more she describes the people around us, the more I believe she's telling the truth. She seems so confident about all of it.

"Who is the man at the table with her?" she asks.

"Ah, I have met him in the smoking room," I explain. "That's Mr. Benjamin Guggenheim. I haven't had the pleasure of meeting his wife, however."

She lets out a giggle. "That's not his wife."

"Oh?"

She nods, chuckling. "His wife is at home with his daughters. That's his mistress, and she lives. He actually helps a lot of the women and children get on the lifeboats." She shakes her head. "But he doesn't survive."

I inhale. It's difficult to believe so many of the rich first-class passengers wouldn't get into boats. "He did seem like a good chap when I met him."

"Other than the mistress, I guess he was—is."

Our entrees are served, and we break the conversation for the moment while I mull it over. Looking around the room, it seems so impossible that such a tragedy will occur, but Millie insists it's true.

The salmon is delicious, as expected, but I can hardly concentrate on the meal with all the questions I want to ask her. I take the opportunity while we await dessert and the others are occupied in conversations again. "You say a ship comes to the rescue."

"Yes, but not until it's too late," she explains. "The *Carpathia* was two hours away when they got the distress call. They came as soon as they could. Some other ships didn't even answer. The telegraph operators I mentioned, Harold Bride and Jack Philips, tried frantically to get help."

"I imagine they would." I pause a moment as a thought comes to me. "Did they survive?"

"Jack didn't, but Harold will make it."

I'm not sure what to make of that. We enjoy our dessert, and I'm happy to have the dinner over with as I want to talk to Millie more without whispering.

Mr. Brandeis rises first. "Will, Edward, would you join us for brandy and cigars in the billiard's room?"

Edward accepts while I think of an excuse to decline. "I'd enjoy the good company, but I'm afraid I've already promised Miss Baker I'll walk her back to her room since she is without a chaperone."

"Very good then," he says.

"Miss Baker, would you care to take a walk on the promenade?" I ask Millie.

"I'd love that." I stand and pull out her chair, bidding farewell to the others. Thankfully, Agatha has accepted an invitation from Mrs. Hippach to join her and Miss Allen, so I needn't be concerned with escorting my sister back to her room at the moment.

We refrain from speaking for a while as we step out of the dining room. With everyone else finishing their meal at the same time, there is too much of a crowd to talk of sinking ships and survivors. Unease washes over me as I think about the level of detail she provides when speaking of the passengers and crew.

Could it all be true?

10

Millie

It was kind of fun for a few minutes being in the rich people's dining room on the *Titanic*, but the reality of it all sunk in as Will pointed out all those people I know are going to die. I'm glad to get away and get some fresh air.

I'm a *Titanic* passenger now. *What if I don't make it either?*

Will holds the door open for me as we step out on the promenade. "We can talk freely out here. Most will choose indoor activities for the evening."

Mr. Astor's laughter rings through my mind. He is completely oblivious to the horror he's about to face going down with the ship into the icy waters. It doesn't help that I know about some of his last moves, which were pretty brave. He may have been a little creepy to marry a woman so much younger than him, but in the end, he will put himself above others.

I don't even notice I'm shivering until Will takes off his jacket. "Here. There's a bit of a chill in the air."

"Oh, thanks." I try to give him a smile, but that's hard when I'm thinking about so many deaths. He offers me his arm again, and we stroll down the promenade. It's crazy how much room there is. They could have easily put more lifeboats here.

"I hope you weren't too offended by our companions' talk of the pool incident," he says. "It's just a highly unusual occurrence, bound to find its way into dinner conversation."

I shake my head. "No, that was fine. No doubt everyone is totally shook from someone doing something that unexpected."

"I... suppose that's accurate." We step up to the railing and both look out to sea. I drop his elbow and put both hands on the cool steel. The ship seems so sturdy. I can see why no one thinks it's going to sink. And it feels so real. If I'm dreaming, this is the most vivid one I've ever had.

Maybe I'll wake up soon, and Mom will be standing over me.

I notice Will seems just as lost in thought as I am. "You look so far away. Do you miss your home? I guess I never asked why you are even on this ship."

He turns to me. "Parts of me miss Southampton, yes. But my siblings and I have been preparing for our new lives for months now."

"New lives?"

He lets out a long sigh. "The situation has been rather difficult since our parents passed."

"Oh, I'm sorry. I didn't know." I place my hand on his arm and hope I haven't upset him.

"No apologies needed," he insists, looking back at me and smiling. "Our mother and father both passed from influenza the year before last."

I shake my head. "That's awful."

"Mother died first," he says distantly. "Father went within the month. I don't think he wanted to live without her."

"That's so... heartbreaking." I don't know what else to say. What a horrible way to go, watching someone you love die first.

"It was—is. Yes, it still is hard to reconcile."

"So, it's just the three of you now?" I ask.

He nods. "Yes. Edward and I struggled in deciding what actions to take. You'll have to forgive Agatha. She took Mother's loss hard. My mother loved her social life, so Agatha has tried to keep us in the same circles. But, finances have been difficult since their passing. Simply put, neither Edward nor I were prepared to run the business as father did."

"And people ignore you just because you don't have as much money?" I know that happened a lot back then. I guess it still happens in 2025.

"Some do, yes." He inhales and lets it out slowly before continuing. "Once our business started to suffer, Edward and I needed a new business opportunity. Our grandfather—on our father's side—needed help in his successful business in America. So, we finally decided to sell the home and the company in Southampton and relocate."

"That sounds so hard, picking up and leaving everything you know." I kind of understand the feeling.

"It is, but we have family and prospects in America." There's so much sadness in his eyes. "It's not that I don't wish to see my grand-parents. It's just that I miss my parents so much, especially my mother."

"You were close."

"Very." He takes another deep breath. "What about you? Your mother and sister were with you when you... ended up here?"

I nod. "Yes. Mom was pretty excited about our vacation."

"And your father?" he asks.

"Dad's been gone since I was about five," I explain. "I remember him, but not very clearly. Mostly I remember the difference in my mother before and after he was gone. She used to smile all the time. Then one day, she didn't. It's hard to get her to smile, even now."

"I'm sorry to hear that." He looks at me with genuine concern.

"Thanks." I swing around and watch the moonlight flicker on the waves. "She did her best with my sister and me. She worked as a wait-ress while she went to law school."

"Your mother attended law school? How unusual for a woman." Will's eyes are wide in shock.

That makes me laugh. "Yes. Women can be whatever they want in my time. There are tons of female lawyers. Mom did well, and that's how we could afford first class on what was meant to be the trip of a lifetime for her. Now, well, I have no idea where she's at–or where I am, I guess."

"Things are quite confusing."

"You've got that right." I look around the promenade deck. "Mom is such a *Titanic* fanatic. She's obsessed, I tell you. I think it all started with the movie, which she saw before I was born. I guess Dad was into it with her back then. They went to museums, collected things, found stuff on the internet."

"Perhaps it still gives her a connection to your father," he suggests.

I look at him, cocking my head. "That's actually... I never thought about that before. No wonder she's so obsessed with anything *Titanic*."

"Obviously, I've never met your mother, so I can only speculate," he says. "But it does sound like it was something they had in common."

"Yeah." I always knew studying the *Titanic* made her happy. I just never thought about why. Now, I may never be able to tell her I understand.

We both stare out at the black abyss for several moments before Will breaks the silence. "So, you say the iceberg rips a hole in the side of the ship?"

I nod. "That's the researchers' best guess, anyway. It's a big gash, and with that and weak rivets, the water gets in, flooding all those compartments as it goes over the bulkheads."

"I suppose that attracted everyone's attention."

"No, not everyone," I explain. "Most people didn't even know what was happening. It's such a big ship, some of them didn't even feel the impact. Some of the staff said the boat had simply thrown a propeller blade. A lot of them didn't even wake up at first."

"I suppose that makes sense," he says.

He's just being polite, I'm sure. Everything I'm telling him must sound completely insane. I guess it just shows what a nice guy he is. I wonder if I'm just dreaming about him and putting it all in a time-travel-to-the-*Titanic* theme. I think I might miss him if I wake up. He's nicer than any of the guys I've met in my life.

"It takes a lot of time for everyone to realize what's happening, and then there's a rush to the lifeboats," I add. "But they insisted on women and children first. So, men put their women in and were never seen again." I lower my voice a little in case someone's around. "Like Mr. Astor." A shiver rushes over me, and I wrap my arms around myself. I don't think it's just from the cold.

"It all sounds terrible," Will says, and I believe he really feels that way about my story–even if he thinks it's just that–a story.

"It is," I agree.

"We'd better get you back to the stateroom," he says. "Come." He offers his arm again, and I take it. It's a little warmer, walking close to him. It doesn't take long to get to his sister's room, where we pause at the door.

I turn to face him. "Thank you for dinner."

"It was my pleasure," he says. "Thank you for your company."

He leans forward a little, and our eyes lock for a second with our faces close together. I can even feel the warmth of his breath. It seems he's going to kiss me, and I'm starting to think I'd like that. I bite down on my lower lip, staring into his eyes.

Will blinks a few times, and then turns away. I take a deep breath– of course a guy from 1912 isn't just going to kiss me in the hallway outside a stateroom. He unlocks the door and backs away.

Disappointment washes over me. A kiss would be pretty bold for 1912. That's too bad. Even if I'm just dreaming, I have a feeling it would have been nice.

"Goodnight," he says with a small smile.

I give him a nod and hand him back his jacket. "Goodnight." I go inside and hear him lock the door behind me, and I lean against it for a moment, catching my breath.

I turn to see his sister sleeping in the bed. I guess tea with the ladies didn't take that long. It looks like the couch is mine. That's fine. It's her bed. There's still one dim light flickering, which I guess she left on for me, along with laying out a fancy nightgown, which was nice of her. Now that I know about their parents, I understand why she's so worried about her brothers. They're all she has left, after all.

I sure hope she doesn't lose them on the *Titanic*. I get a chill just thinking about it. I hadn't considered yet whether Will would live. It's not like I've memorized the names of all the *Titanic* survivors, so I have no idea.

Putting that thought aside before it keeps me up all night, I figure out a way to shimmy out of my dress. With its lower neckline, it's not as hard to undo as that tight-collared day dress.

Changing clothes this many times a day is exhausting. What a crazy way to live.

The corset is the hardest because it's tied in the back, but once I figure out the loop, it's not too hard to loosen it until the damn thing is off. I'm not looking forward to wearing that again. Thankfully, the nightgown is comfortable.

There's a pillow and blanket on the couch, and I fix it so it's cozy and settle into it. It's been very strange and scary being on the *RMS Titanic*.

I hope when I wake up in the morning, I'll be back in 2025.

But then.. I wouldn't get a chance to say goodbye to Will.

11

Will

With Millie safely in Agatha's room, I step into my own, which is still dimly lit. I undress quietly, slipping into my bed clothes before turning off the light and settling in beneath the warm blanket.

But sleep escapes me. All I can think about is Millie. Her stories of the ship sinking seem so fantastic, they cannot really be true. Yet, she tells it all with such conviction, I've found myself floundering between believing every word and thinking her mad.

The latter is more likely the case. It has to be. To think she appeared suddenly from the future would be the ravings of a lunatic, and I don't believe myself to be one.

Perhaps I'm drawn in by her beauty, and that's what makes me wish to believe her. She's truly the most beautiful woman I've ever seen. Her strawberry blonde hair falls in waves around her shoulders. Even when it's contained in an updo, a few strands tend to dangle delicately and attract my attention. Her bright jade eyes are so captivating, especially when they glisten in the light. Even the sound of her voice is as pleasant as music.

All these things captivate me, and perhaps that causes everything she says to seem to be true. One thing I do know is that I will protect her. She's obviously in a vulnerable state, and I've seen the fear in her eyes. I decide that when we get to port in America, I'll ensure she gets the very best care for her mental state.

Yet, I can't help but wonder whether we'll make it that far. What if she really is having premonitions about the ship sinking? Perhaps that part is true.

"I'm not sleeping well either."

My brother's voice startles me out of my thoughts, and I look up to see he's stepped into my room. "I hope I didn't make too much noise and wake you," I tell him.

He shakes his head, adjusting his robe. "No, just an unexplainable feeling of unease. I probably had a bit too much of the braggarts in the billiards room. Care for a brandy?"

"Yes, please." Tossing the covers aside, I reach for my robe. Sleep isn't likely to come soon anyway. Perhaps the brandy will help. "I take it that some of our more difficult traveling companions were there. What was the discussion about this time?"

He hands me the drink. "It was tiresome... mostly just more talk about the pool incident. Half the men were appalled, thinking it a third-class passenger who somehow wandered into the first-class spaces. Many of those complained endlessly about security measures. Sir Duff-Gordon was going on about how they should be locked down below, and if the woman was not now in custody, that he would ensure she was arrested."

My nerves rattle at the thought. The urge to protect Millie seems to come naturally to me.

He takes a sip of brandy before continuing. "Some of the chaps that were there tell the story as if the woman was throwing herself at them. They're certain she was attracted to them and intent on becoming their mistress."

I almost laugh at that because it's so preposterous, but I'm also incredibly irritated.

"I see that look in your eye." He smiles slyly. "And that's why I was glad you'd declined the invitation to join us. You would have felt the need to defend the woman. Frankly, there were more than a few moments when I almost did as well. But I kept it to myself. None of them have any idea Millie is the woman in question."

"I suppose it's best I wasn't there." I take a long sip of brandy.

He takes a drink as well as we both step over to the sitting area to relax in the silk-covered chairs. "Precisely. Try not to pay any of them any mind. For most, it was only the drink talking. The others are harmless. Anyway, Millie seemed to handle herself well at dinner, despite her recent injury. You were certainly engaged in some extensive conversation with her at dinner. What did you discuss?"

I weigh the advantages of sharing her story with him. He'll likely dismiss her as mad, yet I've always been able to talk to Edward about any topic. I see no reason to change that dynamic now. "She believes she is from the future."

His eyebrows nearly touch his hairline. "Say again?"

"The year 2025, to be exact," I continue, despite the look of credulity in his eyes. "I realize how this sounds, but hold your opinion for a moment. Not one man, including myself, saw the girl before she was suddenly in the water. Don't you find it impossible that a room full of men would ignore a scantily dressed woman walking among them?"

"Perhaps, and I do find that odd, but from the future?" He takes another drink. "You must acknowledge that it cannot possibly be true."

"I'm loath to believe it myself, yet her knowledge of the passengers is convincing," I argue. "She was aware that Mr. Astor's young wife is with child. How could she know such a thing unless she runs in the proper circles? She was quite familiar with the life of Mrs. Margaret Brown, and she knew that the young woman accompanying Mr. Guggenheim is not his wife."

"She's not?"

"No, apparently that's his mistress," I explain. "His wife and children are at home. I'm sure some of the New York socialites know that, but if Millie ran in those circles, someone would recognize her."

He takes another sip of his brandy and contemplates this for a moment. "So, most of these people are at the top echelon of society. It's possible to hear talk about their personal lives outside of New York. She probably just reads a lot of those horrible gossip rags. No doubt all that information can be gleaned from them. That hardly means the girl is from the future."

He has a point, but it's not just the social gossip that strikes me as believable. I consider telling him about the ship sinking. That's unbelievable as well, but less so than telling him Millie is from the future.

"I think I'll have one more before turning in," he says. "That should get my mind off everything that's transpired and help with sleep. This is quite excellent brandy, in any case. They've certainly taken care with the liquor selections on this ship. Care for another?"

"Please." Perhaps it will help me sleep as well. He refills our glasses, and we sit quietly for a moment while I decide the best way to tell him about the ship sinking. I know it's for the best that he's aware. That way, we can both prepare just in case there's some truth to Millie's claims. I would never think of telling Agatha, but I do need my brother's awareness to protect her.

I decide the best way to say it is directly. "Millie is also adamant that the ship is going to hit an iceberg and sink."

I'm thankful I've waited until he swallowed to speak, as he begins laughing immediately. "Will, that's preposterous. First she's from the future, and now she's saying this unsinkable ship will sink?"

"I want to think it's ridiculous, but her explanation has merit." I lean back, thinking of all she told me. "Apparently, the side of the ship strikes the iceberg, tearing into it. Due to some miscalculations with the engineering, water overflows the bulkheads despite the sealed compartments, and she flounders."

"That woman spoke of this ship's construction?" he asks.

I nod. "Yes, and she seems quite knowledgeable."

"Well, surely there's an explanation for that," he says. "Most women know nothing of this sort of thing. Perhaps her father is a shipwright."

"No, her father passed away when she was a small child," I explain.

"It's just her, her mother, and sister. She says her mother is quite knowledgeable about this ship in particular."

"How odd."

"It is. Yet, her explanation seems quite plausible." I take a longer sip, nearly finishing off what's left in my glass.

"I doubt that it's even possible," he argues. "You and I have followed *Titanic's* construction since the beginning. It seemed no expense was spared. How would there be faulty engineering?"

"It has to do with weak rivets, apparently," I say. "Perhaps they misjudged the strength required."

He shakes his head. "I hardly think so. As I said, they spared no expense. Why wouldn't they use stronger connectors than necessary?"

All I can do is shrug. "Perhaps they cut corners more than they admitted. It wouldn't be the first time a company has done as much. You and I have seen that in our father's competitors."

"True, but still, this is one of the largest passenger ships ever built. How could she falter?"

"I'm just saying the explanation she gave is plausible." I take the last sip of my brandy, setting the glass on the table beside me.

"I'll give you that," he says. "But all this relies on the word of a woman who believes herself to be from the future. You cannot expect me to believe that."

"I don't," I say. "But our sister's life will be in danger if she's right. Perhaps she has premonitions where she believes she is from the future, yet these visions themselves are true. We cannot completely discount them. It's best to be prepared."

"In what way?" he asks. "Assuming for the moment that the ship will sink, which it will not, what might we do to prepare? We'll ensure our sister and Millie get settled in a lifeboat, and that's all we can do."

I nod gravely. Ship's orders are usually to save women and children first. "Because ships such as this don't have sufficient lifeboats for everyone aboard, that may prove difficult."

"Surely there are enough for the women and children in first class," he argues.

"I would hope so." It seems downright evil to only think about the first class passengers, but I do not draw Edward's attention to his statement.

He finishes his brandy. "And perhaps you've had too much to drink for tonight, as have I. I'm grateful for one thing. This conversation has made me exhausted. No doubt sleep will find me now."

I nod again, hanging up my robe as I get ready for bed. He pauses at the door and turns to me. "Just don't go falling in love with a lunatic, Will."

He turns off the lamp and steps into his room before I can respond. I lie back in bed, staring at the dark ceiling above me. Falling in love? That's preposterous. I'm simply trying to ensure her safety.

Yet, she is strikingly beautiful, and thoughts of her have invaded my every waking hour since I pulled her out of the water.

I'm not falling in love with her, *am I?*

12

MILLIE

I WAKE TO THE FEELING OF A TINY HAMMER KNOCKING AGAINST MY skull. My head is buried under a blanket. Even in my sleep, I must've been trying to keep out any trace of light. I can't remember what I dreamt of, but I believe I saw my mother's face. I do remember every minute of last night's dinner and my talk with Will on the promenade. Was that a dream, or is it my new reality? I don't even want to pull the blanket down and see where I'm at.

Part of me hopes I'm back in 2025. I miss my mom and Ally. What I wouldn't give to see them again! But then, there's another part of me that knows I've already grown attached to Will. If I had to leave him behind, and he truly is a passenger aboard the *Titanic*, I'm not sure I could ever forgive myself.

"We'll be eating breakfast on the deck." The voice I hear is clearly Agatha's, and I exhale. I'm still on the real *Titanic*, and we're yet another day closer to the iceberg disaster. A shiver runs through me, even though I'm not cold under the blanket.

"Yes, milady," a male voice I don't recognize says. I hear the rattle of dishes and what sounds like several people coming and going, and even under the blanket, the scent of fried ham and fresh bread is strong enough to make my stomach growl. Still, I stay put, feeling a little awkward about popping my head out with so many people in the room.

"Will there be anything else, milady?" a woman asks.

"No, that will be all."

I wait for the door to shut before sitting up.

"Good morning," Agatha says. She seems to be in a better mood than usual.

"Good morning." I swing my legs over and sit up.

"Did you sleep well?" Her smile is tight-lipped, but at least she's smiling.

I nod, pushing the blanket aside. "Not too bad."

"I do hope the sofa wasn't too terribly uncomfortable." She tilts her head to the side slightly, as if she truly is worried about my discomfort and not just saying that to be nice.

"It was fine," I insist. "Not bad at all, thanks."

"We'll take our breakfast outside, so we'll need to dress first," she tells me, still smiling a little more than I've seen her do before, at least when she's talking to me. "I can assist you with your day dress."

"Thanks." I'm not looking forward to wearing that scratchy lace neck again, but I'd sure like to eat, so I guess I need to put something on. She hands me a fabric bag full of something first. "What's this?"

She furrows her brow for a moment, but then smiles. "Talcum powder, of course." When I keep staring at her, she adds, "It's to enhance your scent, along with some perfume." I still don't get it, until she points to her underarms. That's right. I don't have my deodorant. It's not the greatest substitute, but it'll have to do.

I almost groan out loud when she pulls out the corset next, but I figure I'll keep my irritation to myself for now. I don't want to piss her off.

Thankfully, she leaves it a little looser than she did yesterday, and it's really not too bad. There aren't quite as many other layers as the dress I wore for dinner, and soon, she's reaching in the closet while I hold my breath. *Itchy lace, here I come.*

But she doesn't pull out the same dress. This one is blue and designed like a suit with a super long jacket, but it's a gown.

"It's fortunate that our sizes are compatible," she says, adjusting it so she can help me slip it on.

"I really appreciate you loaning me your clothes." I push my head through the top, and she makes a few adjustments before giving me the jacket. It looks a little strange until I realize there's a belt to secure it at the waist with an oversize button.

"Think nothing of it," she insists. "You need to be presentable, and apparently, you have no other items of clothing."

I wonder why she doesn't think that's strange. A woman doesn't just pop up on a ship with no luggage out of nowhere. Maybe this is still a dream, and the people my mind has put into it just go along with it. Maybe I dreamed up Will as the perfect guy.

She's already dressed, so she quickly ties up my hair and pins a hat to it. "There, I believe we're ready. Shall we go outside for breakfast?"

I nod, feeling pretty hungry and not caring where we eat.

It turns out they were carrying an awful lot of food out to the deck, at least a lot for two people. The breadbasket is piled high with different kinds of rolls, and there are a few different types of jam. We each have a silver-dome covered plate in front of us, and there are several more around the table, along with a teapot.

"I hope you enjoy omelets," she says. "I didn't want to disturb you when you were still asleep, so I took a guess at what you might enjoy."

"It all looks great. Thanks so much." I place my napkin in my lap like she does and just sort of wait for her to start eating. It's weird having everything be so formal, even something as simple as eating breakfast. I'm used to just grabbing something on the go, or if I'm eating with Mom and Ally, just digging in whenever I want. But now, I'm not even sure I can reach for a roll with my fingers.

After a few awkward moments, she finally starts eating, and I do the same. The omelet is really good, with ham and mushrooms in it and lots of cheese. The rolls take some getting used to because they aren't quite like what I'd eat at home, but they're still good and fresh.

A few minutes into breakfast, Agatha takes a sip of tea and looks at me over the cup. "Are you enjoying the voyage?"

I'm not sure how to answer that. Of course, I'm not. I'm stuck on the *Titanic* not long before it sinks. But I don't think Will has told her any of that. He probably doesn't want her to think he's lost his mind. "It's been as nice as can be expected, considering the circumstances. It's a beautiful ship."

It's not a lie. In a weird way, I feel lucky to be here since people from my time have only seen it on the bottom of the ocean or recreated on a movie set.

"Lovely," she says, taking a bite of her roll.

I do the same and try to figure out what to say next. When I swallow, I ask, "How about you? Do you like being on the *Titanic?*" A chill runs down my spine when I ask the question, knowing what's going to happen. I wonder how many people feel lucky to be on the ship. They won't for much longer.

"It's been lovely." Her expression changes a little, and I realize she probably didn't want to come. She left her whole life back in Southampton, and it's not like she can jump on a plane and visit people whenever she wants to. She's stuck with writing letters or just cutting ties and forgetting the past.

I wonder if I'll have to do the same.

I try to come up with ideas of what women might talk about in 1912. They don't have careers to discuss, at least not the rich women. There's no TV shows, no Internet. I can't imagine what they do all day. "Do you have any hobbies?" I finally ask.

"I enjoy playing music," she says.

"Do you play an instrument?"

"Yes, the piano." Her eyes look distant. "We couldn't bring Mother's Steinway."

"I'm sorry," I say. "That really sucks." She lifts an eyebrow. "Uhm, that's too bad."

"It was my favorite." She takes a sip of tea and closes her eyes for just a second. "But my grandmother has a fine one as well. I'm looking forward to reaching the States so I can play my music again."

"I'm sure that will be nice when you get there." I have no idea whether she's going to survive the disaster, but I might as well be positive. She's a first-class passenger, and a woman, so she might make it to a lifeboat. But I don't know about her brothers.

Will....

If I manage to get back to my own time, I might never know what happened to him.

"And you?" she asks, kicking me out of my thoughts.

"I like to draw." Sort of... I can't exactly say I make digital art and post it on social media.

"How intriguing," she says. "What types of subjects do you specialize in?"

"Um, animals mainly." Half my page is cats.

"Interesting." She's quiet for a while, and I take the cue to eat more. But I soon realize I'm reaching the limit of my stupid corset, so I'd better slow down.

"I understand your mother and sister are possibly aboard some-where?" She seems skeptical, and I can't blame her. "Tell me about them."

They're not on board, and I have no idea what to say to that, so I pretend I'm still finishing the bite I swallowed two minutes ago while I work it out. "My mother loves the *Titanic*, and she's been looking forward to the trip." I can't say she's an attorney. "My sister is two years younger than me. We're very close." Vague answer, but it's all I can give.

She raises her brows but says nothing until her next question. "Where are you from?"

That's easy. "The Midwest, in America."

"I see," she says. "What brought you to Southampton? Perhaps I know some of the people you visited with."

Shit. Will told me she was really involved in the social scene there, and I don't know any names I can drop. "Well, we really just went there to catch this ship."

"You sailed all the way from America to turn around and go back, just to be on the *Titanic*?"

It doesn't make much sense, now that she says it. "Yes."

"And your mother is aboard?"

"Yes, I think so." I try to take a sip of tea, but she's fast with the next question.

"In first class?"

"She should be." I feel like I'm being grilled by a cop.

"Miss Baker, I don't believe that." Agatha's blue eyes seem to cut through me. "I believe your family is below decks in third class, second at most, and that you're trying to get my brother to fall in love with you for our money."

"What? No, I—"

"Would you have me believe that's not the case?" She sets her teacup down so hard it rattles.

"No, not at all… I mean yes, I think." I take a breath. "Look, Agatha, all I want to do is go home. I'm not interested in anyone's money, and I sure don't want to be on this stupid ship."

"I don't believe you."

That's it. My heart starts pounding, and all my nerves stand on end. I get up, scooting my chair back with my legs. "I really don't care what you believe. It's the truth."

"Hardly," she scoffs.

"I don't want your money," I insist. "I don't even know how you live like this. It's suffocating."

"I'm sure it's easier to be loose with the men in third class."

I feel like decking her, but I hear a voice behind me.

"Agatha?" Will says, and I turn around to see him and his brother. "What are you doing?"

"I'm merely trying to get the truth out of the woman," she says.

My eyes go wide. "Truth? I—"

Edward steps over to Agatha. "Perhaps we'll discuss this inside."

I shake my head. I'm done with her.

"Or perhaps it would be better if we step away from this discussion altogether," Will says calmly, though his eyes tell a different story.

Is he upset with her–or does he doubt me, too? "Millie, would you care to join me in a game of shuffleboard?"

"I'd love to." I take one more look at Agatha, who is staring out at sea, and then cross the balcony to will, wrapping my arm around the elbow he's offered. I just need to walk away from her. I can't believe she said those things. I sure don't want any of her money.

I just want to go home.

13

Will

I feel the tension in Millie as we depart from Agatha's room. I haven't heard enough to know what they were discussing, but I can certainly guess.

"I apologize for my sister," I say when we're out of earshot. "It's no excuse for rudeness, but she has felt the need to take on a motherly role where my brother and I are concerned."

"I know, but she really pissed me off."

I raise a brow at the expression. I'm not sure exactly what it means, but it comes across as vulgar... and somehow appropriate. I can't say I haven't felt "pissed off" by Agatha now and again. "I'm sorry."

"I mean, I'm glad she's loaning me dresses," she adds. "That part is nice. But to accuse me of... never mind. I just want to forget it."

"That's for the best idea under the circumstances." I look ahead and notice the shuffleboard area is empty. "Here's where we play."

She shrugs. "I've never played shuffleboard before."

"It's quite simple, I assure you. I can teach you how to play."

She gives me a sideways glance and smiles, her green eyes shimmering in the morning sun. "Okay."

"Here's the board," I say as we approach it. "The object is to simply slide the disks over to that triangle there, which is marked for scoring." I drop her arm, opening a nearby cabinet and retrieving one disk and a stick. "We use this stick to push it along, like this." She stands close while I demonstrate. "You cannot push beyond this line, and the disk must land in the scoring zone to count. Would you like to try?"

"Sure." Before I can get it for her, she reaches for her own stick and disk, even setting the disk on the floor. I'm finding myself less surprised at her independence, which is delightfully refreshing.

Her first attempt slides far off the board, and she erupts in pleasant giggles. "Oops! Let me try that again."

"A bit too powerful," I agree.

This time she uses a lighter touch, but the disk still goes too far. "Here," I say, stepping in. "It's more of a slide than a push." I place another disk then reach in and help her adjust her grip, placing my hands over hers. They are warm, and the scent of her perfume is pleasant. I turn to face her, and her eyes are sparkling with laughter. My heart tingles with excitement as our eyes lock, our faces so close, I'm only inches from touching her lips.

Realizing this, I back away quickly, clearing my throat. "Try it that way." I barely get the words out.

She exhales, her lips pursed together. "Okay." It's nearly a whisper, but she turns away and averts her eyes, focusing on the shuffleboard stick, her aim clear before she pushes it forward. "Yes!" she says as the disk lands square in the middle of the seven-point area.

"Well done!" She smiles at me, and I have to look away again. I busy myself with acquiring a stick for myself, along with a black disk to clash against her white, and gave it a slide, aiming so as to land on the opposite side of the triangle.

"Oh, no. You are not going to just let me win," she protests. "No taking it easy on this girl. Go get that and do it again."

"I'm sorry?"

"I know you did that on purpose." She puts her hand on her hip. "I'm going to beat you fair and square. No cheating to lose."

"I don't believe it's cheating if one loses," I argue.

"Do it again," she insists.

"Very well." I aim straight for her disk, and hit it out of the scoring zone.

"What was that?"

"You insisted on fair play," I counter, my smile crooked and my shoulders raised. "Such are the rules of the game."

"Oh, this is so on." She grabs another disk, obviously aiming for mine, which she taps lightly into a lower score zone. "I could start to like this game."

"Can we play?"

We turn around to see two young boys approach enthusiastically. "Sure thing," she says without hesitation. "We'll team up. One of you play with Will and the other with me."

"I'll play with you," the dark-haired boy says to her.

She smiles at him, her eyes glistening again. "Awesome. What's your name?"

"Tommy."

"Okay, Tommy, we're the white team." She looks at the other boy. "And what's your name?"

"James."

"Okay, James, you get Will. Sorry about that." A sly giggle escapes her lips, and I have to shake my head.

"Oh, we shall see who is sorry." I give her a wink over the boys' heads, and they gather up the disks and get more of them from the cupboard, as well as their own sticks.

"Ladies first," she says, getting into position.

"I see," I say. "So now we're stacking the odds for the girls."

"I'm not a girl!" Tommy protests.

"You're not, so it's not stacking anything." She sticks her tongue out at me, and I laugh as she makes her shot. "That's a score, right?"

Tommy nods. "Eight points."

"Only if it stays," James adds.

"This is true." I take my spot and attempt to knock her disk out of the point zone, but I falter and end up putting her into the ten-point zone.

She raises her arms in victory. "Awesome!"

I have no idea what that word means, but I love the way her face lights up when she says it.

The game continues with each of us taking our turns through several rounds. She seems so at ease with the children, and it's beautiful to watch, especially given our serious conversations and her uncertain state at the moment. I see a glimpse of her heart, full of pure joy and a warm embrace of life. Her smile is infectious, and I find my own heart fluttering.

I can't allow myself to think that way. Either Millie is from the future, which is highly questionable, or she has a serious mental illness.

After a couple of rounds, the game is a draw. "I think I'd better take a break," she says.

"Of course," I say. "You lads continue the game. It was a pleasure being your teammate, James."

"That was fun!" he exclaims.

"Thank you, miss," Tommy says.

"Call me Millie," she insists, "and I had fun being your teammate, too." She smiles at them as we wave goodbye, and they run to gather the disks. Millie turns to me, somewhat winded from the activity, her smile reaching her eyes. "That was fun! Would've been better without this corset, but oh well."

"It was fun." I can't help but let out a chuckle, my heart soaring with happiness. "Would you like to go back to the stateroom to relax?" I see the worry flutter into her eyes, so I add, "My room, not Agatha's."

She exhales. "Maybe later, but I think I just want to walk around a little. It's hot inside with twenty thousand layers of clothes on." I don't wish to discuss women's garments, but I do wonder what she's accustomed to if not the traditional style of dress. Perhaps it's evidence that she's truly not from this time.

I offer my elbow, and she wraps her hand around it. I must admit, it feels good being close to her, especially after such an enjoyable time at shuffleboard. Our connection seems stronger for it.

"You seem at home with children," I say as we stroll along the promenade.

"Yeah, I like kids," she confirms. "I've been a Big Sister since I turned eighteen."

I frown, confused. "I was under the impression your sister was much older than that."

She lets out a pleasant giggle. "No, not that kind of big sister. There's a program where I'm from called Big Brothers/Big Sisters. We team up with kids who need mentors to help them."

"Ah, well, that sounds lovely." It's obvious she has quite a loving nature. "That's kind of you."

She shrugs, looking around. "It helps me, too, not just them. It feels really good to know I've made a difference in their lives."

"I suppose it would." A strong breeze picks up, and many of our fellow passengers hurry inside. "Perhaps we should finish this stroll indoors," I suggest.

"That's a good idea."

I hold the nearest door open for her, and we slip inside where I once again offer my elbow. We walk quietly for a few moments, then she slows to a stop near a staircase.

She looks at the portion that leads downward. "Where does that go?"

"I can't say as I know," I say. "I suppose it goes to C Deck."

"And then lower after that?"

"I suppose." I notice a change in her demeanor, and she becomes very quiet. "What's the matter?"

"Most of them won't make it out."

I feel a chill at her words. "C Deck?"

She looks at me with sadness in her eyes. "Third class."

I'm sure there must be enough lifeboats so that third-class passengers can make it out alive, particularly the women and children. "How is that possible?"

87

"The stewards are going to lock all the third-class passengers downstairs," she explains. "They'll be trapped there until almost all the lifeboats are gone."

"Surely the women and children—"

She shakes her head. "No, most don't make it. A lot of the lifeboats are launched only half full, so they could have held a lot more people if it had been done correctly."

"Didn't the crew give everyone warning?" I ask. "Why don't they ensure that the boats are full?"

"With everyone insisting the ship can't sink, no one was prepared." She inhales, and lets it out slowly, still shaking her head. "The people up in the crow's nest who are supposed to be lookouts don't even have binoculars."

"That cannot be possible," I argue. "Surely, that is standard equipment."

"They didn't have them," she insists. "They could have probably avoided the iceberg completely if they'd been better prepared." When she looks up, I see moisture welling up in her eyes. "Will, all those people didn't have to die. And now here I am in the middle of it all. I just can't—"

The tears begin to fall, and I pull her into my arms, gently rubbing her back as she sobs, her body quivering against my chest. Once again, she's warm and her closeness stirs something in me, but this time, it's the need to keep her safe. If she's right about what she says will transpire, I can't let any harm befall her.

After a few moments, her body stills, and she starts to pull away. "I'm sorry."

"There's no need to apologize," I insist. "This is a frightening situation for you."

She looks back down the stairwell. "Can we go somewhere else?"

"I'm happy to escort you anywhere," I say. "Where would you like to go?"

14

Millie

I needed that cry. Ever since I realized I am on the real *Titanic*, the one that's going to sink, fear and sadness are my constant companions. I guess that's a normal response to ending up on a doomed ship when you know exactly what's about to happen. But being in Will's arms has calmed me down. Now, I feel like I need to get to know some of these people. For some reason, two people in particular come to mind.

"Where can I go to send a telegram?" I ask him, brushing the tears from my cheeks.

Will cocks his head a little, giving me a light chuckle before answering. "Well, I'm fairly sure you cannot send a telegram one hundred thirteen years into the future."

That makes me laugh, and all the tears seem to be gone for now.

"I'll escort you to the radio room." He holds out his elbow again, something I'm really starting to like, and leads me up the stairs to the boat deck, so I stop looking down at the place that triggered such awful thoughts.

We're barely around the corner when we're stopped by a line of people standing in the hallway in front of the radio room area.

"Excuse me, sir," Will asks the man at the end of the line. "Is this the queue for the telegraph office?"

"It is," the man confirms. "Though I must say, it's quite a wait."

Will looks at me questioningly. "I'd like to stay," I tell him.

"Then we shall."

I can't help but wonder how many people in this line will actually survive. Will this be their last communication to their loved ones? I wish I could tell them to say as much as they can to them. But I doubt the ship would let a woman run around first-class telling people the ship is about to sink. With my luck, they'd arrest me and lock me up below deck like they did Leo's character in the movie.

No matter what I do, I have to avoid being placed in the brig.

So, I refocus and concentrate on the wireless operators, trying to remember how things went for them. They were amazing, staying there and sending out messages until water actually flooded the room. I wonder whether I could be that brave.

Finally, we reach the counter. "May I help you?" The man behind the counter looks harried as he rushes us along. He's young, probably about my age, and I'm guessing this is the junior operator.

Will looks at me. I guess I haven't told him my plan, which is that I don't have a plan. I just felt like I needed to talk to these people. "Hello. What's your name?" I ask the operator, trying to sound pleasant.

His eyebrows nearly touch as he stares at me before finally saying, "Harold Bride." So, he is the junior operator. At least he will survive. "Is there a problem, Miss?"

"Is Jack here?" He's the one who doesn't make it. I have no clue what I'll say to him if he's here, but I feel like I have to say something to him.

Harold shakes his head. "No, he's on a break right now. How do you know Jack?"

"It's a long story." It definitely is. I can hardly tell Harold that I'll learn about Jack in about a hundred years only because he died on this very ship.

"Miss, would you like to send a message or not?" Harold asks, but not in a rude way. "I do have a long line of people waiting."

I look behind me, and he's right. "No, thank you. I'll come back to see Jack later."

Harold gives a nod and talks to the man behind me, and Will and I step away. His eyes are wide, but he says nothing until we're clear of the crowd, and then it's a whisper. "You really do know their names. How is that possible?"

"They're pretty famous now," I tell him.

"In the future."

I nod. "Yes."

"I just can't—"

I can tell he's trying to believe me, but I admit the whole thing is insane, so I don't blame him. "They risk their lives staying behind sending as many messages as they can," I explain. "It's because of them that the *Carpathia* comes. Harold is the junior operator. Jack keeps sending messages while Harold gets his life jacket on and gets ready to leave. Then some guy comes in and tries to get Jack's life jacket, and he punches him out. They both try to get out but get separated. Harold helps launch one of the last lifeboats, but he gets washed off the deck, and the boat overturns. About thirty men end up standing on it or clinging to it until a couple of other lifeboats come to rescue them a couple of hours later.."

"You're so certain when you speak of this."

I shrug. "Because that's what happened. Harold lived to tell everyone about it."

"Amazing." We exit back to the promenade, noticing a change in the ship as it slows down. "We're nearing port."

"In Queenstown, Ireland."

Will looks at me. "That's correct."

I have the sudden urge to drag Will off the minute it docks. But would that be the right thing to do?

"If you're concerned about the ship, perhaps it's best for you to disembark," he says.

"I won't go without you," I insist.

"I doubt I could convince my brother and sister."

"Plus, you only half believe me." I wouldn't believe me, either. They have their whole lives on this ship, what's left after their parents' death. I can't expect them to change their plans entirely based on the words of some crazy woman from the future.

"I am trying to," he says softly.

"I know." We lean against the railings and watch the ship sail into port. It really is surreal, being on the *Titanic* in 1912, watching all the excited faces as the huge ship pulls in. I shake my head. "It wouldn't be the right thing, anyway. If Harold and Jack can stay to send messages, I can stay too."

Will puts his hand over mine on the railing, squeezing gently. "You are quite brave."

I don't know if that's true, but I must be here for a reason. Running away now won't help anyone.

Once the ship is secured, and the gangway lowered, people begin to embark and disembark, and some cargo is carried off. I see the Royal Mail clerks pulling along a large cart full of bags of mail, and I wish the clerks could just stay there in Ireland, but I know they won't.

What really bothers me is the happy faces of all the people getting onboard. "Most of these people aren't first-class passengers," I tell Will quietly. "Most of them are already on. There are a few second-class passengers who may have a chance of survival, but most of the hundred and twenty-three people getting on now are in third class, doomed to be locked down below while others escape." It feels hard to breathe. "I just want to scream for them all to turn around and get off."

Will nods. "As do I."

I turn to look at him. "You believe me?"

"Sometimes I do, and other times, it just seems so impossible," he admits. "Yet, if there's a chance at saving lives, I can understand why it would be worth it to try to warn them."

I watch a couple walk up the gangway. They're both laughing and so obviously happy. "America was a dream for these people, a promise of a new life." I look up at Will. "I suppose it's the same for you, Edward, and Agatha."

He nods. "Indeed. Yet life is much more difficult for these people of lesser means. My siblings and I have a secure future not dissimilar to the promises we had in Southampton. I'm quite sure these people expect to work hard and reverse their fortunes in America."

"Probably," I agree. I'm so grateful to see a few people walking down the gangway, though I know it's not nearly enough. "Only seven people get off here."

Will watches the gangway and nods. "I would expect such a low number. Most on this ship are overseas passengers."

"Right." I catch a glimpse of one disembarking passenger who stands out from the others. "Oh, see over there, the priest getting off? He has all that camera equipment."

"I do," he says. "Perhaps his covenant with God has protected him."

"That's what they say because of the message he received," I explain.

"How so?"

"That's Father Francis Brown," I explain. "He's a really good photographer. He's so good, a first-class passenger offered him a job in America."

"Yet he's disembarking?"

"Yes," I say. "He messaged his superior asking if he could go. He got a telegram back saying, 'Get off that ship-provincial!' in all caps. So, there he goes." I watch as Father Brown steps safely onto the Irish dock, and I can't help exhaling with relief. There's one life saved at least. "He already took several pictures of life on the *Titanic*. Those pictures will be very famous."

"I'd imagine so."

"One of his pictures is the last one of Captain Smith alive." It's so hard to think of all the people who will die here.

"How do you know for sure that it's him?" Will asks me.

But just then, a man leaning on the railing not far from us calls out, "Goodbye, Father Brown!"

I hear Will hitch a breath next to me. "Astonishing."

Turning to him, I see his eyes wide. Maybe he's finally convinced. I lower my voice since so many people are nearby, watching the people board. "It's because it's true. The *Titanic* is one of the most famous ships to ever sink. It's real, Will."

I shiver, even though it's warm out, and he wraps his arm around my shoulders.

Another smiling couple walks up the gangway, the man carrying their luggage. It isn't much for the long trip, but I can tell by their clothes it's all they have. Still, they look so happy. "Will, I need to help these people," I tell him. "I know what's going to happen, so that's on me. Maybe that's why I'm here in the first place. I know it all sounds completely insane."

"I must admit it does, but I'm willing to help you in any way I can," he offers. "If that means helping others, then I'll do just that."

"Thank you." I want to cry again as the people keep coming aboard, all of them smiling and happy about the promise of a new future that's actually going to be pulled out from under them.

I have no idea how I'm going to do it, but I need to figure out a way to help all these people.

15

WE REMAIN OUTSIDE UNTIL THE SHIP LEAVES PORT, WATCHING AS THE people on the dock wave farewell to the new passengers. Millie is clearly unnerved by it, and in some ways, so am I. If this ship is doomed as she says, it's quite profound that over one hundred new passengers have boarded her.

For the moment, I'm only concerned with Millie. I decide that getting her away from those wishing a good voyage to their loved ones will do her good. "Perhaps we should return to the staterooms," I suggest.

She nods silently and takes my arm as I lead her back inside. She seems to grow stiffer as we approach the rooms until I realize the source of her apprehension. With all that has happened, I've almost forgotten about her argument with Agatha.

"My sister has her moments, but I assure you, she will be polite now," I say, confident my brother has set Agatha straight. Mother would never approve of her being rude to company.

"I hope so, but I don't know if I can stay in that room with her if she isn't," Millie says.

"I'm not sure what other arrangements could be made, but I will not allow you to be uncomfortable," I assure her.

She looks at me with glistening green eyes. "I believe you."

For a moment, I forget to take a breath, my heart fluttering.

But I avert my gaze quickly and open the door, finding Agatha inside on the sofa. She rises as we approach. "I'm terribly sorry for my behavior earlier," she says. "I'm happy to share the room with you, and you're more than welcome to my gowns."

"Thank you." Millie exhales, relief washing over her face.

"Some of the ladies are taking lunch in the café, if you'll join us." Agatha looks at me. "Edward has agreed to escort us."

"Very well." I stay for a moment to observe them both before determining all is well and excusing myself to my own quarters. I certainly welcome some quiet time to think.

Edward stands adjusting his suit as I walk into his room next door. "Ah, you're back. It seems we have quite a few new passengers. I found the excitement on the dock invigorating. Did you catch it?"

"I did." I settle onto the sofa. "Millie and I watched from the promenade."

"As did I." He sits in the chair facing me. "How is Millie feeling?"

"Well, I believe. She no longer complains of headaches."

"That is good to hear," he says sincerely. "Terrible mess about her disagreement with Agatha. I reminded our sister that Mother always put charity and politeness above all else. She immediately agreed and arranged to include Millie in her ladies' luncheon."

"So, I've heard." I remove my hat and adjust the brim. "I'm glad that's settled."

"And yet I see your mind is, in fact, unsettled."

"It is," I admit.

"I take it Millie is still under the impression that she's from the future?" He rests his elbow on the armrest, and his chin on his knuckles.

"Yes, and she continues to provide evidence of such."

He raises one brow. "Such as?"

"She knew the names of the wireless operators, even one who was not currently in the radio room," I explain. "And then there was a priest—Father Brown—with photography equipment leaving the ship in port. She knew his name and details of his hobby."

"And you believe her."

"Yes."

His eyebrow arches again, but he doesn't speak..

"It's quite compelling," I argue.

"My dear brother." He leans forward. "Millie is a lovely and charming woman. I can understand why you wish to believe her, but you must know the idea of a woman from the future is impossible."

"I know that, and yet she is so certain, her information so detailed." I imagine the confident look in her eye while she's told me these things.

"Agatha has a hunch that this is an act to get close to you for our money," he says. "She thinks maybe she's a third-class passenger who spied on you before her stunt when she fell into the pool."

"No, that cannot be." I can feel rage surging in my veins, but I try to remain calm. I don't think Edward is accusing her of anything untoward, merely repeating Agatha's words. "She wasn't there before I saw her in the water. No one was swimming, and there were no women in the room. She would have been noticed long before getting anywhere near the pool."

He holds up his hands in mock surrender. "Perhaps. Yet to have her appear from the future seems far too unlikely. I only want to ensure you're not hurt, brother."

"I know." There are still so many moments when I falter between thinking Millie is simply in a fragile mental state and believing that she's a woman from the future.

More often now, I find myself leaning toward the latter.

* * *

DRESSED FOR DINNER, EDWARD AND I WAIT FOR THE LADIES TO GET ready. "I can tell you're pleased to dine with Millie again," he says. "And that's quite all right. But please, remember our discussion this morning."

I nod politely to my brother, but inwardly I refuse to be suspicious of Millie. She's clearly not a gold digger. Either she is suffering from delusions, or she is truly from the future. Regardless, she deserves my respect and protection, and I intend to treat her with such.

Once again, I'm not prepared for the extent of her beauty as she walks into the room. This time, she's wearing a royal purple gown with silk trim, the tailored jacket of which appears to have been made just for her, though I know it was not. Her hair, adorned with matching purple ribbons and florals, looks lovely pinned up on the back of her head.

"You look lovely," I say quickly.

"Thank you. And you look handsome." The way she smiles at me seems to light up the room, and I care not whether Agatha and Edward disapprove. I'm positive I know Millie's pure heart.

I offer my arm, which she takes readily, and escort her to the dining room with my siblings following. "How was your afternoon?" I ask her.

"It was fun," she says. "Agatha and I had a good time at lunch with the ladies."

"I'm pleased you enjoyed yourself." And I'm glad my sister has come around. I expected as much. Though she's protective and prone to jump to conclusions, Agatha has a kind soul.

The staff opens the door, and I escort Millie across the dining room to our regular table. Mr. Brandeis and Mr. Hippach rise as we approach.

"Will, my boy!" Mr. Brandeis says boisterously. "I'm so pleased you brought Miss Baker along again."

"I'm happy to see you once more as well," Millie says before I can respond, echoing our more formal language. She holds her gloved hand out charmingly, which he takes and kisses lightly.

"Miss Stewart, you're also looking lovely this evening," he says to my sister, who also offers her hand with the same result.

Edward and I seat the ladies, and the waiter comes forward with menus. This time, I offer one to Millie, who chuckles and takes it, to the raised brows of the men at the table.

"I'll have the chicken tonight, please," she says, and I give my own order while Edward orders for himself and my sister.

"Quite a crowd came aboard in Ireland," Mr. Hippach says when the waiter steps away. "Steerage must be quite full now."

"I don't know why there must be so many of them," his wife complains.

I can feel Millie stiffen and expect her to protest the rude comment. Instead, she confidently steers the conversation away from it. "Eloise, I really enjoyed the tea you brought this afternoon."

The woman's face brightens instantly. "I'm so glad you like it. It's one of my mother's favorites. I just had to bring a supply along with me." She looks at her husband. "You know, the imported spice variety from China."

"Oh, yes," he says, taking his drink from the waiter. "It is quite good."

"Will, you missed quite the chess match this morning," Mr. Brandeis says. "Edward really gave old JJ a run for his money."

"I tried," my brother chimes in with a chuckle. "In the end, I floundered."

"That sounds quite interesting," I say. "I'm afraid I was engaged in my own competition."

"Oh?" Mr. Brandeis raises a brow.

"I believe my brother was busy being bested by Miss Baker at shuffleboard," Edward adds with a wink Millie's way. She responds with a pleasant giggle.

"Guilty." I raise my hand in mock surrender.

"I didn't win," Millie explains. "I believe the game was a draw. And my partner, Tommy, was much better than me."

"I had quite an able partner myself," I add. "James and I did our best."

"I take it Tommy and James were young lads," Miss Allen says.

"Yes," Millie confirms. "It was quite fun. Ladies, we'll have to team up against these gentlemen soon for a game on the promenade."

"Oh, I'd so love that," Mrs. Hippach says. "I cannot wait to best Louis."

All the ladies giggle, and once again, Millie's smile lights up the room. The table's mood is much livelier than it has been all the nights before, with Millie engaging everyone and ensuring they all have an enjoyable dinner conversation.

"I'm so sorry to see this dinner come to an end," Mr. Brandeis says when we've finished dessert. "Miss Baker, I believe I speak for all when I say how much we enjoy your company." He looks at me. "Your classmate is simply dazzling, Agatha."

"That she is" I look at Millie and match her smile before my sister can reply.

"Thank you, everyone," Millie says. "It's been a lovely dinner."

"Well, let's get these ladies escorted to their evening activities," Mr. Brandeis says. "Gentlemen, I'll find my way to the smoking room soon, and you're all welcome to join me."

I know I have no intention of leaving Millie, but I nod politely. She wraps her hand around my elbow, and as we leave the room, her eyes light up.

"Will, can we go someplace different?" she asks.

I let out a light chuckle. "You know I won't refuse, Millie. Where would you like to go?"

Once again, I await her response with wonder. I've never met a woman quite like her in my life, and I can only guess at what she has in mind.

16

I GLANCE AROUND TO MAKE SURE WE'RE OUT OF EARSHOT OF ALL THE dinner guests then lean in and whisper, "I'd like to go downstairs."

"Downstairs?"

"Yes, to third class." I'm not even sure we can get there, but somehow they did in the movie. I'm guessing they lock the gates or guard them to keep people from coming up to first class, but maybe it doesn't matter if we go the other way.

"I don't know if that's a wise idea." His smile fades into a frown.

"You said you'd escort me anywhere I wanted to go," I argue.

"I did."

"And that's where I want to go." I give him my best puppy dog eyes, and he caves immediately.

"Very well." He offers me his elbow again and we head to the exterior staircase, going down several flights until he pauses, holding up his hand then putting his finger to his lips.

"It's a mighty fine mess you've made," I hear a man say gruffly. "Clean it up!"

"But I'm supposed to remain at my post," another complains.

"Do it now or you'd better figure out your swimming legs!"

Will turns to me, gesturing that we should step quietly, which we do. I feel like a ninja as he silently opens a door and ushers me through it, taking more than a few seconds to ensure it closes without a sound. I want to laugh, so I hold my mouth closed while he smiles and shoos me down another stairway.

Once we're clear, I can't hold back the laughter. He takes me by the hand and stays one step ahead of me, checking around each corner. Soon, I hear music filtering up the stairway.

My heart races. "This is just like the movie!" I hurry ahead of him, confident we're clear of any crew trying to stop us.

"I'm afraid I don't know what that means."

I don't bother to answer because I'm already pulling the door open, and a lively party is going on inside what looks like the dining room. "Come on!" I grab his hand and pull him in, smiling at all the happy people. The mood is clearly different from first-class, where I felt like I had to hold back everything I wanted to say or do. Here, people are really letting their hair down.

A man in the corner is playing a fiddle while everyone around him claps, and several couples are on the dance floor in the center. People are walking around handing out huge glasses of beer. Their energy is infectious, and I immediately pull Will into the center of it.

"Dance with me!" I shout over the noise of the crowd.

I spin around, laughing at his wide eyes as he's suddenly thrust into the middle of the kind of party he's probably never even seen before. After a beat, he shrugs, laughs with me, and takes a few hesitant steps, but it's clear early on that his dancing style isn't going to cut it here.

"Here, try this!" I try to show him a few steps, but it's clearly not working, so I lean in where he can hear me better. "Forget all the ballroom dancing you learned. Here, just feel the music and go with it!"

"Like this?" He bounces as he spins me around, which makes me laugh again.

"Good enough!" I take both his hands and look down at my feet.

"Try this!" I'm no Riverdance queen, but I've seen enough social media videos of people having fun with it to fake it. He catches on quickly to that. "I'm impressed!"

The song ends, and we all stop to applaud, then the fiddler starts in on a slow song, and Will pulls me in close, though he still keeps a little distance between us. His hand feels so warm against the small of my back, and we both sway softly to the music. Half the room has calmed into a more romantic vibe, though there are still people throwing dice and playing cards on the other side of the room, some of them loudly claiming victory and others arguing about the results.

I look up to meet Will's eyes and hitch a breath. He's looking at me intensely, as if seeing into my soul. My gaze travels to his lips, which look so inviting, and I can feel my heart pounding in my chest.

But I can't let myself go there.

Clearing my throat, I back up. "Let's go get to know some of these people."

For a brief moment, he looks confused and disappointed, but he composes himself quickly. Of course, in his time, we shouldn't even be thinking about physical contact. He's been pretty good at pulling back those other times we've been close. Something tells me this time he wanted the kiss, but I can't let him get to me like that.

We're on a ship that's going to sink, and I don't know what will happen to us. Even if I somehow get transported back home, I'll never know what happens to him.

The closer I get to him, the harder that will be.

And either way, I'll never see him again.

So, I lead him over to a table with five or six couples. I can tell by their eyes that they recognize us as first-class passengers, but they seem to be welcoming regardless. "Hi," I say to the woman closest to us. "I'm Millie and this is Will. Can we join you?"

"I'm Katie, and aye, that you can," she says pleasantly. "Roger, make use of yourself and get our new guests some beer."

"Aye, but 'tis for the guests," the man who must be Roger answers. He mutters something about a pushy woman as he walks off to get some from a woman walking around with a serving tray, causing me to giggle at their banter.

When he comes back with the beer, Will looks at me questioningly, and I smile to reassure him. I guess none of the ladies in first-class drink beer. "This looks great, thank you!" I tell Roger as he sets the pint in front of me.

"Much obliged," Will says when he hands him his own. "Allow me to reimburse you."

Roger laughs. "No payment needed here, sir. What we have, we share."

"My thanks to you then," Will tells him, holding up his glass with a nod.

I take a sip, a little worried about what beer will taste like in 1912. My eyes go wide. It's a lot stronger than I've ever had before, but it tastes good.

"This is Mary, Ella Jane, and Lilly." Katie points as she introduces everyone. "You know Roger, and that's Liam and Conner."

"Good to meet you," I say at the same time that Will does the same. We make small talk for a bit, then after everyone seems comfortable, I ask, "What brings you aboard the *Titanic*? Where are you headed to in America?"

"Flying by the seat of our pants, we are," Roger says exuberantly. I can't tell if his accent is Irish or Scottish.

"Not true," Katie argues, shaking her head at him. "Ella Jane and Connor have family in New York. We'll all settle near them and see what life gives us."

"Well, best wishes for a happy and successful future, then." Will holds up his glass, and we all clank ours together for a toast, but his words make me sad. All these people are going to die if I don't do something to help them. I take my sip of beer, combing through the *Titanic* knowledge in my brain to figure out something I can do to stop that from happening, something that will help them get out alive.

All I can think of is the locked gates. Maybe there's something I can do about that. There has to be something. I'll think about it, but I don't have long to come up with a plan.

We chat for a while about the places they've left behind and what they hope to do in America. Eventually, the fiddler starts in on a slow song again.

"Connor, spin me a few times," Ella Jane says.

He looks at her and frowns. "Ah, woman! Ain't you had enough of dancin' yet?"

She stands and grabs his hand, pulling him up. "Not yet, husband."

He grabs his beer with his other hand and takes a quick gulp before she drags him over to the dance floor, and despite my grim thoughts, it makes me laugh. The other couples rise.

"Will and Millie, you two should give it a go, too," Katie suggests.

I don't think it's a good idea to get that close to Will again with all the beer we've had. "We'd better get back to our rooms," I say instead.

"Too bad," she says. "Come visit us again, will 'ya?"

I doubt we'll have time before the ship hits the iceberg, so I'm not sure what to say.

"We shall," Will says for me. He slides out my chair while I stand.

"It's been so much fun meeting you all." I smile at my new friends, my heart aching over their uncertain future, especially Katie, who has such a spirit of life in her.

"Don't be a stranger then," she says, laughing at something Roger says to Liam as we walk away.

We retrace our steps, which is a little harder to do with the beer in me, especially the part where we need to be quiet. I remember seeing on some of the documentaries that guards kept third-class passengers from going upstairs, but luckily, that man who was being yelled at before is still gone from his post.

We make it back to B Deck and up to Agatha's door, and I turn to face him. Will's eyes are so blue, lightly glossed over from the drink, though I doubt it's affected him much since he's used to 1912 alcohol. Me, on the other hand…. I can tell I've had a little more than usual.

"I had a wonderful time," I say, my hand still wrapped around his elbow. I don't want to step away from him.

"As did I." He smiles at me, and we're so close, I can feel his warm breath against my cheek. For just a few moments we stay close like that, gazing at each other and saying nothing. The way he looks at me with longing draws me in like a magnet, and before I can stop myself, my lips are on his.

He's so warm, his lips stiff at first from surprise, but it takes only seconds for him to melt into me. His other arm wraps around me and pulls me in as I deepen the kiss and reach in with my tongue to explore his.

Electric sparks of pleasure tingle all over my body as I rub my hands against his back. I savor the way he tastes, with just a hint of strong beer on his tongue, otherwise deliciously sweet, his cologne a pleasant scent of musk and something else I can't identify. The unfamiliarity of it reminds me where I am.

The *Titanic*....

I can't do this with Will, a man I'll probably never see again and always wonder whether he survives the disaster. Having shocked myself out of our moment of passion, I back away quickly.

"Um, goodnight." I open the door quickly and slip inside before he can reply.

I can't fall in love with a man from 1912... and definitely not on a doomed ship in the middle of the Atlantic Ocean.

17

WILL

EDWARD IS SOUND ASLEEP BY THE TIME I RETURN TO OUR ROOM. I CAN hear him snoring from his adjoining room. But I'm not quite ready to fall into slumber, not with that kiss on my mind. I quietly pour a scotch and slip out onto the deck.

My mind has been going back and forth between believing Millie and thinking her mad, but after that kiss, I'm positive she's from the future. No woman in 1912 would be so bold. And if I believe that about her, perhaps I'd better take more seriously her insistence that the ship will sink, as difficult as that is to fathom.

The evening breeze is cool, and my mind shifts to thoughts of icebergs. I believe the water is cold enough here that they might be a concern. I think of all the people on the ship, particularly those souls in third-class who are so hopeful about a better future, those I shared a drink with this very night. I need to help them if I can.

To do that, I need more information.

Finishing the last sip of scotch, I head inside. I hope Millie is wrong about the *Titanic*, but if there's one thing I learned from my father, it's to hope for the best and plan for the worst. I'll need some good sleep tonight to begin those plans.

* * *

"You're up early."

I turn to my brother's voice as he slips into my room. "Yes. I had some tasks I wanted to get done this morning."

"Oh?"

"Just a few items I want to check on." I straighten my hat. "Can you please tell Millie I'll be back shortly?"

"I will," he says. "Anything I can assist with?"

"Not yet, but I'll let you know."

"Will?" he says as I start through the door.

"Yes?"

"Whatever you have in mind, please remember what I said about not getting hurt." He gives me a stern, brotherly look.

"I don't think that's possible for any of us at this point," I say. "But I promise I'll try."

"That's all I can ask for."

I hear him go back to his room as I step out into the hallway and head toward the cafeteria, hoping to find who I'm looking for. I need answers about the ship, and I've decided on the best people to ask. The first is Mr. Thomas Andrews, the ship's builder. He'd have the most information about the capacity of the bulkheads.

As I'd hoped, I found him in the dining room for an early breakfast. "Good morning, Mr. Andrews."

He stops his meal and stands to shake my hand. "Good morning to you... Mr. Stewart, is it?"

"Yes. Please call me Will."

"Will, then." He gestures toward the chair across from him. "Please, join me for breakfast."

"I'd hate to intrude."

"I assure you, you are not." He gives me a pleasant smile and waves the waiter over. "A menu for Mr. Stewart."

I hold up my hand. "No need for that. I'll just be here a moment. I'll be having breakfast a bit later today."

I turn to Mr. Andrews as the waiter leaves. "I'm loath to disturb your breakfast, but I was wondering if you could answer a few questions about the ship."

He sets down his fork. "Of course. Have you reason to be concerned?"

"No… well, not yet," I say. "I've had a troubling theory about the bulkheads, and I'm wondering if it would be possible."

He nods. "Go on."

"The theory is that there could potentially be a breach in the hull that allows a lot of water inside," I explain. "In that case, if water spills over the bulkheads, it could cause the ship to falter."

His eyes go wide but narrow quickly. "Well, that's quite a theory. I can agree that it's theoretically possible, yet the hull is strong. It would take a catastrophic breach to allow that kind of water in, and it's quite unlikely that would occur."

That's all I need to hear—it's possible.

"Also, I personally inspected the bulkheads only yesterday," he adds. "I assure you, they're sturdy and operable."

I nod, standing and offering my hand again. "Thank you, Mr. Andrews. Please, enjoy the rest of your breakfast. I'm sorry to have disturbed you."

"It's no trouble at all," he says, shaking my hand. "Please don't worry about your safety on the *Titanic*. She's quite sturdy and seaworthy, I assure you."

I nod and smile, but I'm starting to believe that isn't the case.

Stepping out onto the deck, I'm pleased to see that it's mostly crew members out at this hour. I stroll among them, working out which person to address for my inquiries.

"I'm not concerned about ice."

I pause, turning my attention to the officers engaged in conversation.

"None of it is large enough to cause concern for this ship." It's the same man who spoke before.

"Perhaps, but it may be best for the captain to observe caution," another man says. "A bit of a slowdown may be in order."

"Nonsense," the first man argues. "We've a schedule to keep. This ship is stout, and the captain knows what's best for her."

So, there are ice warnings, and at least one crew member seems to be dismissing them. I feel a shudder crawl up my spine as I realize things are coming together for just the catastrophe Millie has predicted.

I wave down a steward who is passing by.

"Can I help you, sir?" he asks.

"Yes, if you could answer a question." I lead him to a lifeboat, and he follows. "This lifeboat... could you tell me its capacity, please?"

"Yes, of course," he says. "I assure you, these are a sturdy lot. These are the standards, and they hold sixty-five to seventy people. We also have some collapsible boats. Each of those holds an additional forty-nine passengers."

"Very good." I notice his keychain dangling from his belt. It doesn't look secure. "And could you tell me the procedure for which passengers get onto the boats first?"

He gives me a relaxed smile. "Oh, there's no need to be concerned, sir. I assure you, the first-class passengers will be the first to board and be sent away. Not that it will be necessary on this fine ship."

Exactly what I was afraid of–first-class passengers first. I'll need to take measures to protect the third-class passengers if Millie's prediction comes true. Now, I need to distract him. "Could you tell me how they fasten?" I point to a life jacket hanging behind the man.

"I'm sure there'll be no need to use them, but here, let me demonstrate." As he turns to take one off its hook, I quickly grab his keys and slide them into my pocket. He doesn't notice. "You slip it over your head thusly." He demonstrates, and I watch carefully so I can get the jackets correctly fastened on Millie and my sister, as well as any others I might assist.

"Well, that seems like a simple process," I tell him. "Thank you for your time. This has been quite reassuring."

"I'm happy to help." He walks cheerfully away, thankfully not checking for his keys, which I feel as I place my hand in my pocket. Hopefully, among them are keys to the gates Millie says will be locked down below as the disaster strikes.

I consider the steward's words as I walk back inside. How cold and callous it is to prioritize human life by how much money one has? Yet, I see it happen in so many ways. Father was always adamant about only doing business with companies that value their workers of every stature. If he were here to see such disregard for life, I can only imagine his response.

I must do all I can to help these people.

Anxious to tell Millie about the keys, I quicken my pace back to the room, only to be stopped in the hall by Mr. and Mrs. Hippach.

"Will, what's the rush?" he asks with a chuckle. "Goodness, man. You look so serious. Is there a problem?"

"No, not at all." I paste on a smile I'm not feeling at the moment. "Mrs. Hippach, you look lovely today."

She smiles at the flattery. "Why, thank you."

"Would you join us for breakfast?" her husband asks. "And Miss Baker, too. Where is she?"

"I was just heading back to speak with her," I explain. "I don't know if she has breakfast plans, but if not, I'm sure we'll catch up with you in the dining room."

"Very good," he says. "Quite a head chef they have aboard this ship. I have sailed on many, and the food is never quite this delicious."

My nerves are rattled. I need to get to Millie to explain my plan. I manage to nod in agreement, but that's all.

"It is very good," his wife agrees. "I do hope you and Miss Baker will join us. She's such a joy to converse with."

I force another smile. "That she is, and I hope to join you both soon. If you'll excuse me...."

"Of course," he says. "We'll see you shortly."

I walk at a normal pace until they turn a corner, then speed up again. From what Millie has told me, the accident occurs on the four-teenth, which is only two days away. We'll need to have a solid plan in place before then. It's possible these keys don't unlock all the gates, so we may have to secure several more before then.

I reach my room and head inside. Edward is gone already, no doubt at breakfast. Knocking on our connecting door, I get no answer, so I go inside.

It's empty.

No doubt they're at breakfast, too, I try to tell myself. Yet, I cannot know that for sure. I look around the room, and there's no sign that Millie was ever here. She has no belongings, only borrowed items from my sister, so there's nothing to reassure me that she's here and will return.

I feel panic rise in me. *What if she is truly gone, back to her own time?*

For a moment, fear envelops me as I collapse into a chair. If she is gone, at least she will avoid the ship's sinking. For that, I should be grateful. But I already feel an ache in my heart. Were she to disappear from my life entirely, I'm sure it would be too much to bear.

I no longer doubt the growing feelings I have for her. As much as they may lead to pain, I cannot deny them.

I hurry off to the eateries, praying I find her in one of them with my brother and sister.

18

Millie

"I'm sure you'll enjoy the Veranda Café," Agatha says. "It's quite charming."

"I haven't been there yet," I admit. "I'm sure it's really nice."

I'm feeling comfortable, too, because today's day dress isn't scratchy like the first one. It's a pretty light blue color with a neckline not quite as high as that other one. Still, I'm in the stupid corset again, but Agatha has kept it loose. I can't figure out why women in 1912 think they need these things. The first day I wore it tightly, I could barely breathe.

Will isn't with us, and it makes me uneasy.

Edward seems to sense that as we stroll down the hallway toward the cafe with me on one of his arms and Agatha on the other. It's strange how I'm getting used to being escorted around like this, though I wish I was locking elbows with Will.

"Will was very sorry he could not be here for breakfast." He's explained it already, but I still don't feel right. Anxiety fills me as I wonder where he is. "It seems his errands were urgent."

"I wonder what errands he had." I also wonder if Will is avoiding me. I can't believe I kissed him. None of these women in 1912 would do something like that. He's probably trying to figure out how he's ever going to face me again—or if he even wants to.

"He wouldn't elaborate, but he won't be long," he says. "But that's more time for me to chat with you lovely ladies."

Agatha smiles as we enter the Veranda Cafe. She was right. It's really nice. It's like an elegant garden setting, with wicker chairs and tables and designs around the windows that look like vines growing up a trellis. It's bright from the natural morning light, and the décor would actually make a really good café even in 2025. I wonder if I'll ever get back there.

Edward seats us both, and the waiter comes over, handing him the menu.

"I really liked the omelet the other day." There's some weird stuff on these menus, so I want to be sure I get something normal.

"That sounds lovely," Agatha agrees. "I'd love to have the same."

Edward orders for us, and a server comes over with some tea. I've never liked warm tea, but it's an everyday beverage here, and I'm starting to like it, especially in the mornings.

When the food comes, it's delicious, as usual. We chat about the décor and the food as we eat. Edward finishes up just as Mr. Brandeis waves at us from across the room. Edward waves back and sets his napkin on the table. "If you ladies will excuse me, I have something to discuss with Mr. Brandeis."

"Sure," I say, and Agatha nods. I watch as Edward walks over and gives the man a friendly handshake then sits with his back to us.

"So, Millie," Agatha says, and I turn to her. "I've noticed how Will has been looking at you recently."

Instantly, I feel heat rising in my cheeks. I'm sure she didn't see the kiss. *Did she?*

"You were home quite late last night," she adds. "Where were you off to at that hour?"

I figure there's no sense in lying. "We went to meet some of the people in third-class."

She raises a brow. "Isn't that dangerous?"

"No," I insist. "Everyone is really nice down there, and we had fun. You can ask Will, and he'll agree."

She nods, setting her fork down. "I no longer wish to be rude, but I feel the need to be straightforward with you. If you are doing something to mislead my brother, I must promise that I will personally destroy you."

Unlike before, the threat doesn't get a rise out of me. I'm glad she loves her brother so much that she'd defend him like that. "I'm not, I promise. I only want to go home."

She lowers her voice to a whisper. "And that would be to the future?"

My eyes go wide. I hadn't realized Will had told her.

"Edward told me about it," she explains, seeing my surprise.

I guess Will told him. "I know it sounds crazy."

"And this is why you couldn't explain about your mother."

I nod. "Yes."

"He mentioned you believed you were on a similar ship." She takes a sip as if we're just talking about our next knitting project. I don't know if I'd be so calm about it if I were in her shoes.

"Yes, *Titanic 2*." I look around, and no one is close enough to hear me. "My mom and sister were with me. They were right next to me and—"

"And you found yourself here."

I take a slow breath, nodding. "And now, I'm starting to have serious feelings for Will."

Her eyebrow arch again.

"But that's not very smart. I have a life back in 2025, and he's... here." I feel a knot growing in my stomach just thinking about it.

"I suppose that would be quite difficult." Her tone is sympathetic and seems genuine.

"I don't even know what's happening back in my time." I push my last few bites of food around on my plate, but suddenly, I'm not hungry. "Maybe I disappeared right before their eyes. Or maybe I'm in a coma, and they're waiting at the hospital for me to wake up. I don't know how I got here, let alone whether I'll ever get to go back. I love my mom and sister, and I miss them so much."

Memories flood my mind, images of all the most important points in my life flashing before my eyes, all of them with either Mom or Ally. I don't want to cry in the middle of the café, but I can feel the tears starting to well up at the thought of never seeing them again.

I guess my choice is either lose them or lose Will. I don't think I can handle either one.

I use my napkin as a tissue to try to keep the tears in, and Agatha pats me on the shoulder. "I understand the pain of loss, believe me," she says.

Sniffing, I nod. "I am super sorry about your parents."

"Thank you." Her mouth turns down, and she suddenly looks as grieved as I feel. "It was so terrible, watching them descend into sickness."

"Will said you brought in the best doctors." In my time, people the age of her parents probably wouldn't die from the flu. I've heard of older people dying from it, or people that were already sick. I can't imagine having to stay in a time when so many illnesses could kill a person.

"We did, but even they couldn't save them." She shakes her head. "I don't like to think of them in that state. Will tells me to remember the good memories of them, and I try to most of the time. My mother was such a wonderful woman."

"Tell me about her." I blink a few times and wipe away the last stray tear before taking a sip of my tea. I've managed to dry my tears for now.

"Oh, she was lovely." Agatha flashes a nostalgic smile. "She was always very stylish. Even when she didn't wear her newest dresses, she'd style them in such a way that the other society ladies would follow suit."

"She was a trendsetter." I think about all the fashion influencers on social media. Maybe she would have been like them.

"Hmm, I suppose that's true." She inhales deeply, closing her eyes for a few seconds before looking at me again. "She was also a true talent on the piano. When I was a very young girl, I'd sit and watch her, dreaming of one day being as talented as she was. She saw my interest and began teaching me. I was only five at the time."

No wonder she misses the piano so much. I don't think I would have been able to leave it behind. But it would probably cost a lot of money to bring a heavy item like that onto the *Titanic*. I guess they really did lose a lot moving to America.

"Tell me about your mother," she says, wiping a tear of her own off her cheek.

"She's wonderful." I have a clear picture of her in my mind, holding her phone and wanting that picture. I hope someday I get the chance to tell her it's not her fault I hit my head. I should have been more careful. "She likes to shop for new clothes, too."

Agatha smiles.

"And she works so hard." I look around to be sure no one's listening still. "She's a lawyer."

"Edward told me that as well," she says. "That's quite impressive. And it's interesting that women can pursue such a profession in the future."

"Women can do anything," I say. "There are even female astronauts."

She shakes her head. "Pardon? I've never heard of such an occupation."

"Astronauts are people who fly into space," I explain. I wonder how much of this I should tell her. I don't know if she'll survive the disaster or not, and if she does, maybe she shouldn't know too much.

Her eyes are wide, as I expect. "That's extraordinary."

"There's so much more." I give her a smile. "The world is a lot different in the future. Though, in some ways, it's the same."

"I suppose it is." She pauses for a moment. "What about your sister? Tell me about her."

"She's younger than me and kinda crazy." I realize that might not mean the same thing to Agatha as it does to me. "Oh, I mean she's silly and fun-loving, not insane."

She nods. "I see."

"We're pretty close," I continue. "We wear a lot of the same outfits even."

"As do you and I," she says with a smile.

I let out a light chuckle. "Yeah that's true. I guess we're like sisters, too, right now."

"And as long as you treat my brother with the respect he deserves, I'm honored to be like a sister to you."

We just sort of smile at each other, and I feel that warm connection, like I'm having a conversation with Ally.

After a few moments, she breaks the silence. "Edward did explain about... the ship." She looks around. "Honestly, I can't say whether or not I believe you about that, but I will do anything I can to help, just in case."

"Thank you." It's good to have someone else on my side.

"Ah, there you are." I turn to see Will, his face lit up with a warm smile. He doesn't look embarrassed to see me, or like he wants to run and hide from me. In fact, he looks relieved to find me here. Somehow, I just instantly feel that everything will be all right.

I hope he enjoyed our kiss as much as I did. From the look in his eyes, it looks like he did.

19

WILL

MILLIE LOOKS SO LOVELY IN HER LIGHT BLUE DRESS, IT TAKES MY breath away for a moment. Though expected, I'm disappointed that my sister is with Millie as I have so much to say to her privately.

"Will," Agatha says, startling me out of my thoughts. "I'm afraid we're almost finished with breakfast."

"That's quite all right." My gaze turns to my sister. "I'll take an early lunch instead."

"Nonsense," she argues. "You need your breakfast. Millie and I will be leaving soon for the morning activities, so you can have the table."

"Oh?" Millie looks surprised as she turns to her.

Agatha smiles at her. "There are quite a few new ladies' activities, and Mrs. Hippach asked if we'd like to participate. Under the circumstances, I understand if you don't want to...."

"No, that sounds cool. We may as well take the time to enjoy what we can." Millie looks at me. "Did you want to talk to me about something, Will?"

I do wish to speak with her, but I don't want to interrupt any cordial interactions between her and my sister. "No, please go on and enjoy yourselves. I can escort you to the activities."

"We'll be going to the reading and writing room," Agatha explains. She gazes at Millie. "Are you ready?"

Millie nods. "Sure."

I assist with their chairs and offer both arms, noticing my brother across the room with Mr. Brandeis. "I'm escorting the ladies to their morning activities," I explain to him as we walk by, heading for the grand staircase since the room is on A Deck. He nods as we pass.

It feels wonderful having Millie on my arm again, even though I'm not able to speak with her alone just yet. I doubt Agatha believes she's from another time, let alone that the ship will sink, so I don't want to worry her about my plans for ensuring the gates are unlocked during the disaster. Undoubtedly, she will find the idea dangerous, if not foolish.

We arrive at the room, and I open the door, Agatha stepping in first to greet the many ladies already gathered there.

Millie turns to me. "We'll talk later."

"Indeed." I nod. "We have much to discuss." I give her a smile to reassure her, wondering if she's been second-guessing her decision to kiss me. I hope she has not. It confirmed the growing feelings I've been having for her and let me know that she is feeling the same way. "Enjoy your morning."

"I will." She gives me a smile that reaches her eyes as she steps inside and is immediately greeted by the ladies. For a woman from the future, she has fit into the social circles in my time very well. It's not surprising with her charm, grace, and kindness.

I turn from the door and step away. It will feel like a long day without Millie by my side.

* * *

I ADJUST MY HAT AS WE WAIT FOR THE LADIES TO STEP THROUGH OUR communal door that evening. Their activities lasted well through the lunch hour, so I haven't been able to speak with Millie alone all day.

And tonight, it seems our calendar will be full once again, with a party being held by Mr. Ismay in the lounge this evening.

"You look splendid." I chuckle at my brother for fussing with his suit more than usual. "I'm sure that young lady you've been visiting with will say the same."

I see the blush rising in his cheeks. He can never hide that from me. "Do you think so?"

"Of course," I insist. "That's one of your finest suits."

I'm just about to add another teasing remark when the door opens and stops me. My heart flutters as Millie walks into the room wearing a lovely royal blue dress, her green eyes sparkling like jewels. "You look stunning, Millie."

She smiles, and it reaches her beautiful eyes. "What, in this old thing?" She laughs, and I quickly understand her meaning.

The sentiment is charming, and it makes me chuckle. I offer my elbow. "Shall we?"

"Yes, we shall." Her warm hand wraps around my arm as she smiles up at me, and for a moment, I can't remember where I am.

Dinner is pleasant, if not a bit hurried as everyone is anxious for the gathering. "I hope you'll allow me to escort you to the party," I tell Millie.

"For sure!" she agrees. "There's nobody else I'd rather go with." There's a flash of pink in her cheeks, and memories of our kiss flood my mind again. Thankfully, Mr. Brandeis asks me a question that takes me out of such distracting yet pleasant thoughts, and I'm able to control my emotions again.

After we've finished dessert, I help Millie with her chair and offer my arm. "Are you ready for the party?"

"Yes," she says. "It's going to be very fun to go to a party on the Titanic."

"I suppose it will be." I watch my brother fetch Miss Evans from her parents' table and wait for them so we can walk together.

"Miss Baker, may I introduce Miss Evans," Edward says when they approach.

"Please call me Millie," Millie insists.

"It's very nice to meet you, Millie. I'm Edith." The young woman smiles warmly at Millie, and they begin to chat as we stroll down the hallway.

We reach the lounge on A Deck, and staff members at the double doors open them for us.

"Wow." Millie looks around, taking in the surroundings. A quartet is playing softly on the side of the room. Several couples are already ballroom dancing, and others sit off to the side, mostly separated in groups of men and women, though a few conversations are mixed.

"This is a bit different than the festivities below," I whisper in her ear.

She chuckles. "A lot different, but it's really awesome to be here. It's kind of the first-class version of it, I think."

I nod. "A fair assessment. Would you care to dance?"

"I'd love to." She seems to be uncomfortable with the dance at first but easily follows my lead. I look into her laughing eyes, hoping it can stay like this forever. I don't know what will happen when this ship sinks, but I feel the urgent need to stay near this woman, no matter what happens.

The song ends far too quickly, and we're swept by the crowd to a table occupied by some of the people we've mingled with throughout the voyage. Mr. Lindquist, a man I've met in the smoking room, draws us into his conversation. "Will, what do you think of these wireless communications onboard?" he asks.

"I'm afraid I don't know much about it, but it seems rather miraculous technology," I say.

"Geoffrey, I'm sure the ladies here would prefer a different topic so we can all converse," another man says.

"The wireless technology on this ship is quite advanced." All eyes turn to Millie. "The Marconi system is the best in the world in this time... now, that is. Its range is a thousand miles, and the antenna runs from bow to stern."

The men in the group are stunned into silence, and I smile wide. She even sounds like she belongs here–for the most part.

"That's… fascinating," Geoffrey says. "How do you know so much about wireless, Miss…."

"May I present Miss Millie Baker," I say in introduction.

"Miss Baker," he repeats.

She shrugs. "I'm just interested in that sort of thing. Wireless tech will be huge."

"Will it, now?" another man asks.

"Yes." She turns to him. "There are a lot of advancements right now. Even using SOS is new."

"SOS?" a woman asks.

"It's an emergency signal," Millie explains.

"I thought that was CQD," Geoffrey muses.

Millie shakes her head. "SOS is faster and more efficient, so that's the newest standard."

"How fascinating." Soon, the conversation shifts, and we have a moment with others engaged elsewhere.

"Millie, would you like to sit?" I ask her, offering a chair at a nearby table.

"Yes, thank you."

Pushing her chair in, I sit beside her. "You're making quite a splash," I whisper.

"I hope I didn't say too much."

I shake my head. "I wouldn't worry. They'll likely forget soon given the upcoming events."

She gazes at me and tilts her head slightly. "You believe me?"

I nod. "Yes, I do, and I have a plan. We can discuss it more later."

"Okay." We turn toward the quartet, which is beginning another lovely song. Millie watches them play, and her eyes sparkle from the moisture that begins to pool in them.

I wave over the waiter, who pours us some champagne. "We should enjoy this night."

She nods. "We should." We toast each other and take a sip then turn back to the conversation at the table.

But not long after, I realize that I want to take advantage of every moment we have left by spending it alone with her. I cannot forget the way I felt this morning when I thought she had possibly disappeared from my time. "Would you like to take a walk?" I ask her.

"I'd love to."

We say goodnight and take our leave from the party, strolling slowly down the hallway. We reach the exterior door, and I lead her out on the promenade. The night is somewhat cool, but there's not much wind.

I walk her over by the railing where fewer people are standing nearby. "I need to tell you something, Millie," I begin. "I don't know what the future might bring... I mean, even though I know the *Titanic* will falter, I don't know what will happen to us."

"Neither do I," she says sadly. "I know a lot of survivors' names, and yours... isn't familiar."

I nod. "It may be that I perish, and that is why I want to spend as much time as I can with you now. I'm falling for you, Millie Baker. I suppose I've known it from the start, but the more days I spend with you, the stronger those feelings become."

She exhales deeply before speaking. "Will, I'm catching feelings for you, too. But we can't think like that. I don't know what will happen to you or me... and I still want to go back to my family in 2025."

I take both her hands in mine. "Then, we must enjoy every second we have together for now." I look into her eyes as I move closer, leaning in to press my lips against hers. She hesitates for a moment then relaxes as I deepen the kiss.

After a moment, she pulls back, gazing into my eyes silently before she seems to work out a decision. "Come with me," she says, pulling me gently by the hand.

Of course, I follow, quite willingly.

20

I PULL WILL ALONG WITH ME AT FIRST. IT'S CLEAR HE'S CONFUSED FOR A
moment, but he eventually keeps in step with me as I lead him back to
his room.

For a woman who came back in time and should know everything
about the *Titanic* in 1912, I'm terrible at knowing what the future
holds. I don't know why I'm here, or if I'll die along with so many
other people on this ship. I don't know whether Will is going to die or
whether anything we do over the next couple of days will change
anything about the future as I know it.

But I do know, from the way my heart races when I look at him,
the way delicate tingles of pleasure touch every nerve when his hands
are on me, and from the powerful draw that I feel when looking into
his eyes that I'm done catching feelings for Will Stewart.

I'm already in love with him.

Even the slightest touch of his hand, warm and strong in my own
as we make our way back to B Deck, feels right. This is the way it
should be.

It's possible we only have forty-eight hours left to be together, and we need to make the most of it. I interlock my fingers with his and squeeze tightly as we make our way up to his door. His brow furrows in confusion for a moment, but he opens it, and we step inside.

"What is it?" he asks when we're alone.

I just shake my head, smiling and squeezing his hand for a moment before I let go.

I'm getting much better at undoing my dresses, and after quickly locking the door behind us, as well as the connecting door, I reach back to unbutton everything.

"Millie—"

"We have two days, Will."

His eyes go wide. "What are you doing?"

I get all the buttons undone and slip off my long sleeves, letting the dress pool on the floor. "We have to make the most of the time we have together," I explain. "I have no idea if we'll live or die. For all I know, I could be whisked back to the future at any moment."

It takes him a beat, but his eyes soften and he nods lightly, his eyes flicking down toward my chest. "Is this what women are like in the future?"

I let out a chuckle as I move in close to him. He's going to need to help me with the rest of the layers. "Only when we're in love."

He hitches a breath, his gaze looking up to meet mine. I swallow at the intensity in his eyes, and he draws me in with his arms. "I love you, Millie Baker. This is a feeling I've never had before."

I nod, swallowing as my heartbeat gets faster. "I feel the same way, so we can't waste this chance to be together."

"We won't," he whispers gravelly as he brings his lips to mine. His kisses are so light at first, but then he deepens them, and I feel his arms tighten around me, his hands wide open as if to touch every inch he can reach. I wrap my own arms around his neck, reaching up to deepen the kiss even more.

This kiss is so much different from our first one. I was pretty tipsy then, still coming down off the excitement from the party. But this... this is just Will and me, completely enveloped in each other for this moment, all those feelings that I have built up for him rushing out as I bask in the knowledge that he feels the same way about me.

His hands lower, and he works to undo the corset, and I feel the heat rise in my core with his hands so close to my bare flesh. I reach for his jacket button and our kisses part for seconds at a time as we pull off each piece of clothing. When almost all of our clothes are off, I lead him toward the bed.

Locking my hand in his, I lean back, scooting up onto the bed and lightly pulling him with me as he tucks the pillow behind my head. We lay for a moment just gazing into each other's eyes. I savor every second. Everything else around us—this giant sinking ship, the decades of time maybe lost to me forever, the many differences in our lives—fades into the background, and all I see, think about, or feel is his hands on my body and his eyes looking at me as though I'm the most beautiful creature on earth.

He pauses for a moment, resting one arm on the bed and placing his other palm on my cheek, his thumb softly stroking my lips and his eyes locked on mine. His breathing is calm, yet I can feel the exhilaration in him. I can hear his heart pounding like mine is even though there are several inches still between our bodies.

A gentle smile forms on his lips as he moves closer, those lips replacing his thumb as he kisses me. I let my eyes close even though I don't want to take them off him for a moment, just so I can feel him against me without the distraction of vision. The intensity of our hearts beating together erupts in a soft, breathy moan that escapes my lips. He responds by parting his lips and deepening the kiss, his tongue gently dancing against mine as my core warms deeper in response.

I don't want to wait anymore, so I tug down his silk boxers, the last piece of cloth between us besides my chemise. He removes them in one motion and comes back down to kiss me again, and I start to explore the smooth plains of muscle that make up his pecs, sliding my hands down his firm back and stopping just short of grabbing his perfectly sculpted ass.

Will lifts up and looks me in the eyes, as if asking permission, before my nod allows him to lift my chemise up over my head. He lets out a whispered moan as he takes me in. I don't feel self-conscious at all having his eyes roam over my bare body. In fact, I feel like I'm exactly where I'm meant to be.

He caresses my breasts while trailing kisses down my neck. This is not lust but love. I see it in his eyes. He looks at me as though he's appreciating a rare work of art he will cherish forever.

"I don't want to hurt you," he whispers.

"You won't," I assure him, though, judging by what I can feel against my thigh, he's definitely the biggest man I've ever been with. Yet, I'm completely confident he'll be gentle.

He enters me slowly as though he's still afraid of hurting me, and I rock my hips to encourage him. "You'll let me know if I need to stop?" he asks me midway. I nod, and he slides in further.

Once inside, he reclaims my lips. I've never felt so completely connected to another human being in my life. We move gently in a steady rhythm, roaming hands feeling each other everywhere we can reach. Our rhythm picks up, and I let go more than once, calling out his name loudly while warm tingles of pleasure erupt over every inch of my body.

I open my eyes to see him staring at me intently, nothing but love in his eyes. He places his palm on my cheek again gently. "Millie." He says my name like I'm a priceless treasure, still gazing into my eyes as I feel his own pleasure erupt inside me.

The next time he calls out my name, his voice is deep and gravelly.

When we're finished, he lays beside me, and it takes several moments to calm my breathing. He pulls me gently toward him in the meantime, and I lay my head on his chest, listening to his quick heart-beat gradually slow into a calm, relaxed rhythm as mine does the same. He pulls the blanket up over us, and I feel safe and warm in his embrace.

I've never felt so bonded with a man. I didn't know feeling like this was possible. I suppose this is what it's like to be truly in love.

"I love you," he tells me again, as if reading my mind.

"I love you, too." I trace my finger along the muscular wall of his chest.

"I want to do everything I can to help you save lives on this ship."

I pause, lifting myself onto my elbow so I can look into his eyes, then I kiss him again as if drawn by a powerful magnet.

When I pull back, I ask, "How?"

"I've already lifted a keyring from a steward to give to our friends below deck," he explains.

I inhale, my eyes going wide. "You stole his keys?" I can't help but chuckle at the thought, and he joins me. I've never seen him look so relaxed and happy.

"I suppose that's what I did." He tucks a stray strand of my hair behind my ear. "I love the way you care about people, and I want to be part of that."

I nod and settle back down with my head on his chest. "We should get some more sets of keys," I say. "That way, we can give them to people whose rooms are in different parts of the ship so they can unlock different gates."

"I agree."

We lay quietly for a few moments, his hand lightly stroking my bare back. "Do you want to go back to the couch in Agatha's room or stay with me tonight?" he asks.

"I want to stay with you," I say instantly. I find his hand with mine and hold it close. "I want to make every moment count."

"And that's exactly what we'll do."

I close my eyes and relax against him, letting his steady heartbeat lull me to sleep.

21

Will

THE FIRST THING I SEE WHEN I OPEN MY EYES THE NEXT MORNING IS Millie's beautiful face. The angled light from the window filters over her, giving her a soft, angelic glow. She looks so peaceful, I don't wish to wake her, yet I do want to begin discussing plans for the sinking with my brother and sister.

So, I disentangle myself from her warm, comfortable embrace and slip out of bed, turning to see her merely adjust herself sleepily and fall back into deep slumber. I get dressed then quietly open the door adjoining my brother's room and slip through it.

"Will," he says the moment I shut the door behind me. "I was just about to wake you. Agatha is quite upset. It seems Millie never returned to their stateroom last night. Do you think it's possible she somehow went back through time?" A chuckle escapes my lips before he finishes his sentence, and he looks at me with a frown and furrowed brow. "Well, that's not quite the reaction I was expecting."

"I know where Millie is," I say simply, grinning widely.

"Where?" he asks, then he gazes at me for a moment, and I can see the realization in his eyes. "I see," he says then, his brow raising slightly. "I suppose it's fitting that I didn't come into your room to offer a midnight brandy last night then."

We're both chuckling now. "I suppose not," I tell him. "We'd better go tell Agatha she's safe."

"Goodness, I'll leave that news for you to deliver."

I suppose Agatha will have quite a reaction, so suddenly I'm not in such a hurry to explain it to her, though I shouldn't leave her in a state of concern. We walk out to the deck, where Agatha is at breakfast, and I see the worry in her eyes.

"Millie is safe," I say immediately upon seating myself.

"Oh, thank goodness." She exhales with relief. "Where is she?"

Edward gives a chuckle, and I send him a sideways glare before addressing Agatha. "She joined me in my room last night, where she is still resting."

Agatha's eyes go wide, but after a few moments, she shakes her head. "I suppose I shouldn't be shocked at anything anymore, given that I've accepted the fact that a woman has suddenly appeared from the future."

"By a means unknown," I finish for her. "Which means neither of us has any idea how much longer we have to spend together."

She lets this simmer in her mind for a moment. "I suppose you're right. I'm just glad she's safe for now. I took the liberty of ordering you some breakfast."

"Thank you." I lift the silver cloche and begin to eat my eggs and biscuits. "On the subject of safety, I did want to discuss something with you both."

"Yes?" Edward asks, taking a bite of his eggs..

"Knowing what we do about Millie's... origin," I begin, "I believe we should act on other aspects of what she has told us."

"About the ship," Edward offers.

"Precisely." I take a sip of my coffee. "I believe we should act as if it will, in fact, go down."

"Certainly," Agatha agrees. "But what can we do toward that end?"

"We could take some measures to try to prevent it, for one," I suggest. "Perhaps we could see that the crew is equipped to spot the iceberg. Also, we could do more to assist those who are at greatest risk of perishing in the disaster, such as those in third class."

"How are they at greater risk?" Agatha asks, her eyes wide again.

"Apparently, several gates across the ship will be locked in third class to ensure more first-class passengers are loaded in lifeboats." I take a slow breath, still loath to admit such practices are at all possible in civilized society.

She puts a hand to her chest. "Good heavens. How is such a thing allowed?"

All I can do is shake my head. "I don't know, but Millie insists it will happen, costing hundreds of lives."

"I can't believe the crew would have such disregard for life," Edward says. "There are women and children below decks."

I nod. "Many of them, so I believe it is up to us to assist."

"How can we help?" Agatha asks.

"I've secured a set of keys from one of the stewards," I explain.

Edward lets out a chuckle. "My dear brother is a thief."

Surprisingly, Agatha is quick to chastise him. "Under the circumstances, we can't blame him. It's for the proper and gallant protection of women and children."

"I only jest, Agatha," he insists.

"My plan is to acquire several more sets throughout the day," I explain. "Millie and I will take them to our acquaintances below so they can be prepared."

"We're both happy to help." Edward nods firmly. "I think Agatha and I can distract one or more of them so we will have several sets."

"Perfect." I finish eating quickly, hoping to accomplish some other tasks before going to wake Millie. "Do tell Millie I'll be back shortly?" I ask Edward once I've finished.

"Of course," he says. "We'll wait here and ensure she receives a breakfast plate."

"Thank you." I leave for the dining room first seeking out any officers and catch two just finishing breakfast. "Excuse me."

They turn and offer cordial smiles. "Can we help you, sir?"

"Yes, thank you." I think of the least confrontational way to inquire. "I have an interest in the business that supplies these lifeboats." It's the first thing that comes to mind. "Might I inquire which officers are responsible for their use and upkeep?"

The brown-haired officer chuckles. "There's hardly a need for their use."

"All the same, could you direct me to the right man to speak with?"

The other man chimes in. "You'll want to consult First Officers Lightoller and Murdoch. They're responsible for all activities concerning the lifeboats."

"Thank you," I tell him. "Do you know where I might find them?"

The other man speaks up again. "I saw them both out near the bow before breakfast. Whether they're still there, I don't know."

"Thank you," I say. "You've both been most helpful."

"Our pleasure." They both nod and smile before returning their attention back to breakfast.

I hurry out to the bow area, hoping they've lingered. Happily, I find two officers speaking with some of the crew. Hoping it's them, I wait for them to finish.

"Can we help you, sir?" one asks as they dismiss the other men.

"Would you be First Officers Lightoller and Murdoch?"

"We are," the other answers. "I'm Murdoch, and this is Lightoller. How can we assist you?"

I paste on my most neutral expression before inquiring. "Ah, wonderful. I wanted to inquire about the procedure for the lifeboats."

Lightoller chuckles, and Murdoch follows suit. "Sir, I assure you there won't be any reason to bother with the lifeboats aboard this ship," Lightoller tells me. "The RMS Titanic is stout and sturdy, I assure you. She's quite unsinkable."

If he only knew. "I'm certain she is. Seeing these boats here over the last few days, I've simply found myself curious as to how such a thing as that would function, should it ever be needed, perhaps on another ship. How are they lowered into the water?" I decide starting with questions about their seaworthiness will take the focus off the questions I truly want answered.

"I see," Murdoch says. "Well, yes, they're quite standard for ships of this size. See over here." He leads me over to the ship's railing to a crane. "We run winches off these davits here, which are already attached to each lifeboat. One each on the bow and stern keeps her steady."

"Interesting." I pretend to examine the mechanism. "How many men does it take to lower each one?"

"We have teams of eight to ten men," Lightoller explains.

"So, there would be teams of men here loading passengers." I can only imagine the panic in the crowd. "I suppose the training for such a thing isn't done often, since it won't be needed on this ship."

"Not a run-through, no," Murdoch confirms. "But we do have the policies in place. I'm in charge of running the starboard side, and Lightoller here would be handling the port. I assure you, we know our procedures well, should an emergency arise."

I hold up a hand. "Oh, of course. I'm completely confident in your maritime abilities." Truly, I'm growing less confident by the minute. "So, loading the passengers, is there a priority?" It seems a good time to bring up my true concern.

Murdoch nods confidently. "Well, our crew uses the standard of women and children first, as do many other ships. We'd probably load the women and children from first class first, then second."

It's precisely what I expected to hear, and it's quite disturbing. I have to force myself to keep my expression from turning sour. "Certainly. But suppose there are people standing by from other classes. In an emergency, would you not simply put them on the boat?"

"Yes, well, I suppose we probably should in an emergency," Lightoller confirms.

"Oh, of course, I don't doubt you would," I say. "I'm confident that no crew members on this fine vessel would be so negligent as to not load as many passengers as possible."

"Of course not," Murdoch agrees while Lightoller nods. "These boats can hold up to sixty-five grown men. We wouldn't dream of sending them away less than full if there are passengers nearby who want to board."

"Quite interesting," I say, trying to act nonchalant. "Well, gentlemen, it's been a pleasure. I have enough information to discuss this with my colleagues. I believe they have some interesting ideas about lifeboats." I offer my hand to both of them.

"Happy to be of service to you, sir." Murdoch takes my hand, followed by Lightoller.

I turn to leave but only take two steps before turning. "Oh," I add. "I've been overhearing talk of ice in the water. You might want to be sure the binoculars in the crow's nest are where they're meant to be. Wouldn't want the boys to miss spotting a 'berg."

Lightoller nods. "I'll be sure to check on that."

It's all I can do for now, so I bid them farewell and make my way back to B Deck. Once out of sight of the first officers, I catch a steward's attention.

"Say there," I say, waving. "Could you tell me the time?"

"Of course, sir." He looks at his watch. "It's 8:34 A.M."

"Thank you," I say, patting his back and lifting his keys, slipping them into my pocket. I do the same in the hallway with another steward before reaching my room.

I'm anxious to get back to Millie to work on our plan.

22

I feel different tonight, my nerves so frazzled it's hard to focus on the dinner conversation, but I try to be polite to all the nice people I've come to know at this table. Late tomorrow night, the ship will strike the iceberg. It feels like the emergency has already started with my fight-or-flight response on high alert. Sneaking a sideways glance at Will, I can tell he's feeling the same way.

After what seems like hours, we're finally done with dessert, and everyone stands to leave. Miss Allen leans in when it's our turn to say goodbye.

"Are you feeling well tonight, Millie?" she asks.

"I'm fine, thank you, Elisabeth." I try to give her an authentic smile. "I've just been thinking of my family tonight." It's not a lie, but not exactly the truth, either.

She smiles sympathetically and pats my shoulder. "I understand. It's always hard to leave my parents and sister behind when I go to the States. My aunt and cousin are wonderful, but it's not the same."

We chat for a few more minutes before Will offers me his arm. It's easier to talk to Elisabeth knowing she will survive the disaster, but I can't help but wonder whether even she will make it if more of the third-class passengers are saved.

Am I sacrificing her life for theirs?

"Is anything the matter?" Will whispers as we step out of the room.

"I'm fine," I assure him, but I'm not sure the answer is true. "Let's just get the keys." The plan we discussed earlier in the day is in motion now. We have a total of ten sets of keys, thanks to Agatha and Edward's help. Now it's our job to get them downstairs.

"I hope no one's blocking the way," I say as Will takes them out of his dresser drawer. "We got pretty lucky last time."

"We did, but I have a plan for that," he assures me.

It's not as fun sneaking downstairs as it was last time. All my giggles and silliness are gone, replaced by trembling hands and a fast, pounding heartbeat. We get down the same stairway all right, but a man stops us right where we avoided one last time.

He puts up his hand. "I'm afraid this way leads down to steerage," he says. "You wouldn't want to go down there... lots of miscreants and thieves, I'm afraid."

I didn't think my heart could pound harder, but it does. As panic sets in for me, Will addresses the man calmly. "I don't doubt there is," he tells him. "But it seems the lady has discovered a distant cousin is aboard and feels a duty to provide her with information about a deceased family member."

"I can't vouch for your safety when down there," the man insists. All my hope fades until he continues, "But I'll be on duty all night. Come up the same way, and I'll be sure to let you through."

"Thank you, my good man," Will says, shaking his hand.

"Thank you." I barely get the words out. I can't believe that worked. I'm sure we wouldn't get the same results if we were from third class trying to come up.

We head down the stairs and hear music again. The same room where the party was held before is bustling with activity. Looking around, I know that even if we save some of them, many of these people will die for the lack of lifeboats, even if they're full. The *Carpathia* will just be too far away.

But we have to try.

"Will and Millie, good to see 'ya." We turn to see a smiling Roger with two beers in his hands. "Come and join us for a pint!"

"Of course," Will says as we follow him to a table and greet Katie and the others.

"I'll get 'ya your drinks," Liam insists, leaving before we have a chance to stop him.

"We don't have much time to drink," I explain. "We're down here to tell you all something important."

"Oh?" Mary asks, giggling. "This sounds so serious."

"I wish it wasn't, but it is," I continue. "We heard the stewards talking about locking all the gates if there's an emergency." Gasps erupt throughout the table. "We couldn't let that happen." I nod toward Will, who pulls out a set of keys. "We need to make everyone down here understand what to do at the first sign that anything's wrong."

Katie looks at me carefully as though she's searching for something in my eyes. "You think there will be an emergency." It's a statement, not a question.

I nod. "I know there will be, and I can't explain why right now. But I need you to help us distribute these keys throughout the entire ship down here. And it's very important… you have to tell everyone to go upstairs immediately at the first sign of danger."

Katie nods, a grim look on her face. "In the old country legends, the goddess Brigid foretold the future. I can see her spirit in your eyes." She turns to Roger. "We need to see to it that all are warned."

He turns to us. "Aye, but language may be a problem for many down here. I do know of a lad who speaks English and Norwegian."

"Find him," Katie says. "Conner, your friend who speaks Lebanese…."

"I'll get him," Conner says, standing.

Will hands the first set of keys to Katie. "We have ten of these, and you'll need several people in charge of them in different areas of the ships. I'm afraid there are several gates throughout."

The translators arrive, and we explain the same thing to them. "We need everyone to know tonight," I tell the group. "Please, have everyone look for the gates now so they know where to go to unlock them."

"We have some Chinese families down the corridor," one of the translators says. "I don't think they speak English."

"The young girl does," Mary says. "I've spoken to her."

Katie nods. "Find her, and we'll help her warn her parents without scaring the child." She turns to us. "Thank you for this. We'll get everyone informed tonight and ensure they all know what to do. Despite what others might think, I believe you."

"It is quite urgent." Will hands her the rest of the keys. "I trust you can distribute these in the manner you think best."

"'Course, I can." She puts them in the pockets of her dress, and I can't help but think about the difference in our clothes, with hers so much more practical. Mine are designed for someone who has so much more wealth. I hug her tightly, hoping she'll make it off the ship. I have a feeling she will, but she's also so stubborn, she may make sure everyone else is off, sacrificing herself.

I hug every one of our new friends, even the men, who seem shocked by my behavior, but I just can't leave without saying a proper goodbye. Finally, Will takes me by the hand and leads me back up the stairs. I want to cry, but we still have to deal with that guard.

"Good evening," he says as we approach. He nods at me. "I take it the news has been delivered." I guess crying is appropriate now anyway.

"It has," Will confirms. "Thank you, sir."

"My pleasure." He nods as we step away, hurrying up the stairs.

"We've done all we can," he assures me once we're out of earshot.

"I know." I inhale to fight the tears. "They're all just such wonderful people."

"That they are," he agrees, squeezing my hand and interlocking his fingers with mine. "You have saved a lot of lives today."

"*We* have," I correct before adding, "I hope so." We can't get to the cabin quickly enough, and as soon as we're there and he locks the door behind us, I fall into his arms crying.

The feel of his strong arms around me is comforting, but the faces of all the people I've met flash before my eyes. I can't help but wonder who will live and who will die. Will hands me his handkerchief when we finally part, but I stay close to him, his right arm still wrapped around me protectively.

"It's so unfair." My eyes meet his. "Why does this have to happen?"

"No one can answer such questions," he says softly. "But we have taken measures. I've told them to ensure there are binoculars for the crew, and the first officers have assured me the lifeboats will be fully loaded. Perhaps that will change the situation for the better, and more people will live."

"God, I hope so." I do feel a little better. No one was prepared before, so maybe these changes will make a difference.

His gaze is so warm and loving, my emotions shift. We have time alone together again, and I should think of it as a gift. If we've prevented the disaster, maybe that means my work here is done, and I'll go back to my time tonight and never see him again.

I press my lips to his, closing my eyes to feel the intensity. He quickly responds by deepening the kiss, his free arm wrapping around me to hold me close. This time, I'm even more anxious to feel him inside me, to completely connect with him in possibly our last moments together.

The clothes come off so quickly and easily, I barely register who removed what. But we're in bed again in seconds, my bare skin against his, our kisses deep and desperate and our hands roaming each other needfully.

But after a few moments, the frantic movements still, and he showers gentle kisses along my neck and down toward my breasts, leaving tingles of pleasure along the way. He pulls himself up before he gets any further, balancing himself while he gently caresses me, his eyes gazing at the contours of my body before meeting mine again.

"You are so beautiful, Millie."

Heat stirs in my core, and I move my hips in response, spreading my legs apart, not wanting or needing anything more but to feel him inside me again. He obliges, gently stroking me with his fingers as I feel the moisture pool for a moment before he slides in easily.

His lips are back on mine in an instant. We kiss deeply, fervently, desperately trying to extract all the feeling out of every moment as we make love. It feels so right, like every moment of my life has been leading up to this one, this connection with Will... this love for him.

When we finish, I rest against him again as he helps me pull the blankets over us. The world may be coming to an end for many of the people aboard this ship, including us, but for now, we're safe in our warm cocoon, our legs and arms intertwined in this moment of togetherness.

The sound of his heartbeat soothes me, and as I drift off to sleep, the last thing I hear is Will's deep voice whispering, "If it's your destiny to return to the future, I wish I could go back with you."

23

W<small>ILL</small>

I<small>T'S STILL SOMEWHAT DARK WHEN</small> I <small>AWAKEN, BUT MY KNOWLEDGE OF</small>
the events that will unfold tonight won't allow me to sleep any longer.
It's April 14, and if Millie's predictions are correct, the ship will hit
the iceberg tonight.

I know Millie needs all the sleep she can get to be alert this
evening, so I slowly slide out of the bed, ensuring she's not disturbed.
I get dressed quietly, and she doesn't even flinch as I make my way
across the room in the faint glow of the first light and take care
opening my brother's door, closing it quietly behind me.

He's still asleep, so I shake him gently. It takes more than one try
to urge him out of his slumber.

"Will?" He blinks and grabs his pocket watch off the side table,
squinting to read it in the dim light. "It's 4:00 A.M." He begins to sit
up, pulling the blankets off. "Has something happened already?"

"No, not yet," I assure him. "Yet, I do need a moment alone to
speak with you."

"Very well." He stands and retrieves his robe from the closet. "I suppose it's too early for scotch."

"Not under the circumstances." I go to his liquor cabinet and pour us both a drink, handing one to him. I take a long sip, studying my brother's familiar face. "I want you to make sure you get Agatha off this ship."

"Yes, of course I will do that," he says. "I'll get her into the first lifeboat available."

I shake my head. "What I mean is that I want you to get on that boat as well, whether I'm there or not."

"Will, I can't—"

"You have to," I tell him.

"But I'll be taking someone else's seat, a woman or a child." He swirls the drink in his hand. "I couldn't possibly do that. And I most certainly cannot leave you behind."

"You must," I insist. "Can you imagine what life would be like for Agatha without us?"

He nods, swallowing his sip. "I see your point, but she will have our grandparents."

"We haven't had much more than correspondence with them since we were children," I remind him.

"True, but they are caring people," he points out.

Shaking my head, I think back to our most recent loss. "You saw how affected she was when Mother and Father died," I add. "Can you imagine her horror at losing both of us as well?"

He inhales deeply and lets it out slowly. "I see your point. Still, that argument holds if she loses only you… and I would feel the same."

"I will do what I can to survive as well, but I must help others," I insist.

"What of Millie?" he asks. "Does she intend to get off the ship quickly?"

"That's why I'm depending on you to assist Agatha," I explain. "Millie will probably want to be sure the third-class passengers are able to get out and that all the lifeboats are loaded properly. You see, I cannot simply leave her to do that alone."

144

"I see the problem." He rubs his forehead. "I promise I'll take care of our sister, and that if I'm allowed, I'll accompany her."

"Thank you." I take the last swallow of my brandy. "I have one more request of you."

"Which is?"

My eyes meet his. "If I don't make it off, I need you to do me a favor."

"Will, don't talk like that," he argues.

"Please," I beg. "I need you to promise to do this one thing."

He exhales, nodding reluctantly. "Fine. No promises yet, but I'll listen. What is it you want me to do?"

* * *

WITH THINGS CLEAR BETWEEN ME AND MY BROTHER, I HURRY TO THE pool room and am happy to find it unlocked and open. I keep the light off and work in the glow of the sunrise through the bow window to test my theory, taking off my suit to reveal the swim trunks I've put on underneath.

My first experiment is with a single lounge chair to determine its buoyancy. Finding that it does, indeed, float, I use pieces of rope I've brought in my pocket to attempt to tie two of them together. Perhaps the girth of several will make an effective raft. After some failures, I'm glad to see that's the case, as the makeshift raft holds me afloat, though not without getting me wet. Even with the chill of the icy waters, at least it might assist some who have no chance at a lifeboat. I get the raft out of the water and hurry to change out of my wet swim trunks and back into my regular clothes before anyone sees what I'm up to.

Jogging outside, I rush down the outside stairwell, skipping every other step until I'm below deck, finding the same guard posted at the third-class entrance.

"Dear man," I tell him before he can say anything. "I hope you can help me. My lady friend lost a prize necklace last night down below decks. I'm hoping to retrieve it."

145

He shrugs. "Well, if one of the passengers down there has found it, you can rest assured she'll never see it again. But I suppose it can't hurt to look. I'm on my post for another hour, so make it quick."

"Thank you, good man," I say, rushing through the door and down the stairs where breakfast has begun in the main dining hall. I scan the crowd for our friends but see no familiar faces until Conner waves me over from the far corner.

"Will, what's the rush?" he asks. "You look as though you've fallen overboard."

He says it with jest, yet I feel the weight of the words. "No, I was testing a theory in the pool upstairs, one that may save lives."

"Save lives?" he asks. "Is this about the trouble you've suspected?"

I nod. "Yes, it is. I want you to pass some information along to everyone down here. It seems that some of the lounge chairs will float."

He lets out a chuckle. "Float? Do you suspect this sturdy ship will sink or something?"

I exhale, wishing this all weren't true. "Yes, Conner, unfortunately, I do." His eyes go wide, and I try to think of a plausible explanation for my knowledge. Having heard from my former visits that most of the people down here are quite superstitious, I come up with an idea. "You see, Millie is able to communicate with spirits. She's had a vision of the ship sinking this very night. I truly need you to act on this."

He puts a hand to his chest as though trying to absorb the shock. "She thinks the ship will go down? Tonight?"

I nod. "She does, and I have every reason to believe her. She's never been mistaken before. That is precisely why we brought you the keys last night. Have you located the gates and distributed the keys?"

"Aye, though everyone is a bit baffled as to why," he confirms. "And now I know. This is quite grave. How will we get all the people to the upper decks and into the lifeboats?"

"That's a good question," I say with a nod. "What's worse, there aren't enough boats to accommodate everyone." His eyes go wider as I continue to explain. "I've been trying to come up with a solution.

Thus, the information I've shared about the lounge chairs. It seems one can tie a few together to create a sufficient raft.."

"Lounge chairs?" He shakes his head. "There's nothin' like that down here."

"I suppose not," I say. "It would take too long to bring them up anyway. There are plenty in first class to make several rafts. Just take them off the decks. Here." I walk up to a regular chair to demonstrate. "These aren't exactly the same, but I've discovered that if you attach them here and here, and continue in a line, they hold together."

He nods. "I see."

"I can't show you precisely on this one, but the backs attach to each other right in the center, sort of right here to right here." I bring two chairs together to demonstrate.

"Got it," he says. "I'll make sure everyone is aware. But I must warn you, we're going to have some frightened people down here today. I needn't explain how many of our people are alarmed by the power of speakin' to the dead. And you say Millie can do that?"

"She can," I lie. It's the only way I can explain it that will get the man to listen.

"How will I keep all these people from tryin' to find their way upstairs as soon as they find out?" he asks.

I hadn't thought of that. "That would result in chaos, and it could cause the captain to issue orders of arrest." I put my hand to my chin and think. I certainly wouldn't blame anyone for wanting to get a jump on securing a lifeboat. I know I'd do the same to save Millie, or if I had any children, I'd want to be proactive for their sake. "Discuss this with Katie and Roger before anyone else," I suggest. Those two, particularly Katie, seem to hold particular sway with the people down here. They can probably control some of the panic.

"A fine idea," he agrees. "People tend to listen when Katie speaks."

"And that could save lives," I say.

He nods. "Show me where to connect them again. I don't want to get it wrong."

I demonstrate again, explaining some of my failures in the tests above deck. "It's important to tell them that people will still get wet.

147

They won't sink, but the waters are very cold. It will be difficult to balance the layers needed to stave off the cold with becoming too weighed down by the ocean once a person is afloat."

He nods again. "Good to know." He pauses for a moment and looks at me. "Did Millie know how long we'll have to get off?"

I feel a chill go up my spine as I remember some of the details Millie has shared. "The ship hits an iceberg. You may not feel that, so stay alert, and Millie and I will try to get down here to warn you. We have only a couple of hours after that to act."

"That's not much time given how many are aboard ship." I can see the fear in his eyes.

"I know." I pat him on the shoulder. "I wish I could do more. It's urgent that you speak with Katie and Roger immediately."

"I'll go wake them now," he says. "We all had a late night."

I shake his hand. "I'll do everything I can to help."

"You're a good man, Will," he says just before I step away.

I hope what we've done is helpful and that Millie and I will help more of these people survive. Without knowing what else I can do, I head back upstairs.

"Did you find it?" the guard asks as I pass.

"Hmm?" I'd forgotten the story I told him, but as his bushy eyebrows furrow, I suddenly remember the make-believe necklace. "No, I'm afraid it's lost."

"I knew it," he says. "You can't trust any of those people down there."

I walk away, amazed at the callous nature of the man's beliefs. I don't know whether he will survive, but I hope he will so that he learns the terrible costs of such thoughts of superiority.

I hurry back to my room, anxious to see Millie again.

I hope we both survive this day, but one thing is for certain, I have to make sure Millie is safe—no matter what becomes of me.

24

Millie

I CAN BARELY HOLD MY HANDS STEADY, MY NERVES ARE SO SHOT. THIS IS it—April 14—the day the *Titanic* will sink. Maybe everything we've done has somehow changed what will happen, but we won't know until tonight. I wouldn't be able to get through the day if it weren't for Will. Though I woke up without him earlier, I know he was busy doing more things to help prevent some of the tragic loss of life.

Now, we all attempt to eat breakfast, but I barely get down more than a few bites of toast.

"You should eat, Millie," Will insists. "You'll need your strength later."

"Maybe for lunch." I set down my napkin and shake my head. "Right now, I just... can't."

He nods sympathetically, reaching below the table to take my hand. "Okay, but promise you'll try again later."

"I will." I inhale, forcing all my focus on his soothing warm hand against mine.

He turns to his siblings. "Edward, Agatha, I want you to get to bed early tonight so you're rested up for the long night ahead. We'll wake you when it happens."

"And I pray you never need to wake us," Agatha says, shaking her head.

"We've already planned for an early evening," Edward confirms.

Will nods at his brother before he turns to me. "Let's take a walk," he suggests.

I rise and give his brother and sister tight hugs before taking his arm. Even if the ship doesn't sink, I have a feeling this is my last day with them all. I'm going to try to enjoy my time with Will all I can. The thought of leaving him makes my stomach sink.

We stroll along the promenade for most of the morning, and as promised, I get down as much food as I can at lunch in the café. "I'd like to see some places indoors that I've missed," I tell him when we're finished.

"Very well," he agrees, leading me to the nearest exit.

"Isn't there a gym on board somewhere?" I ask.

He nods. "Yes, up on the starboard side of the Boat Deck." He leads me up the stairs toward the room. "It's after one o'clock, so it will be time for the children's activities."

"Can we go in?"

"I don't see why not." He opens the door and leads me in.

It's strange seeing all the old exercise equipment, though some of it is similar to what we have now, like the rowing machine and the bikes, which look strange but seem to work the same way. We watch the children enjoy it all for a while, especially a contraption called the mechanical horse, which is the most popular piece of machinery. They're having so much fun, I forget myself and laugh with them for a moment.

"Hey, you're our teammates!"

I turn to see Tommy and James running up to us. "Hi, there," I say, bending down to give them quick hugs. "Are you having fun?"

"Yes!" Tommy says enthusiastically. "The horse was the best!"

As they both talk about the equipment, I can feel the tears welling up in my eyes. I haven't memorized the survivor list, just a few names that caught my eye over the years. I don't know whether Tommy and James will make it.

Will catches sight of this, and I meet his understanding eyes. "Boys," he says. "It looks like the horse is free again. You'd better go get another ride."

"Okay!" James shouts with glee as they run over toward the machine.

I lean into Will, steadying myself in his arms. "I don't want to go to dinner tonight," I whisper. This is all too much. All I want to do is be alone with him and get ready for what's likely to happen later tonight.

He seems to understand, nodding as he leads me away and back to the stateroom.

We don't waste any time stripping off our clothes when we get there. "This may be our last time together," I say as I turn to face him.

He shakes his head, placing a finger on my lips softly. "We don't know what the future holds. But we know we have this moment." He brings his lips to mine, deepening the kiss and wrapping his arms around me tightly. He reaches down, swinging my legs up to carry me to the bed, barely taking his lips off mine for a moment.

I savor every touch as we make love. Every stroke of his hand against my skin, every thrust of his pelvis against mine, every longing look in his ocean eyes. When we finish, I gaze into his deep blue irises that seem to penetrate my soul. "I love you, Will."

"And I love you, Millie," he says, stroking my cheek. "I wish I could go with you."

Moisture wells up in my eyes. "I… I don't think that's possible."

He rolls me over on top of him and holds me tightly as I cry. I try to calm myself out of it, but I hear the ticking of the grandfather clock in the room.

"It's getting late," he says. "We should get started on the rafts."

I nod reluctantly. I want to lie here with him forever, but we still have to do everything in our power to make sure as many people survive as possible.

"We'll get some rafts made with the deck chairs first," he suggests.

"I've shown Conner how it's done, but I fear the people won't have much time."

"And we could have them ready now, assuming no one tries to stop us," I surmise.

"Precisely," he says, getting dressed.

"I'm not wearing a corset for this," I insist. "Give me a pair of your pants."

He raises a brow but does so without argument. They're huge on me, long and baggy since he's so tall and muscular, but he manages to poke an extra hole in a belt, and I roll up the bottoms so it'll be easier for me to move. I put on one of his shirts as well before throwing my dress over the top to hide it all.

We gather up the rope he's cut for the deck chairs, and I take his hand as he leads us toward the promenade where most of the deck chairs are located. It's way past dinner, so there aren't many people here, but we wait for a few stragglers to head inside before we get to work.

There's not much time left.

Quickly, he starts to put some deck chairs together and shows me where they need to be fastened. I'm not the best with knots, but I make sure they're all secure knowing that countless lives will depend on them.

"What's the meaning of this?"

I freeze at the sound of the angry steward behind us, but Will remains calm. "We're doing an experiment, which you'll not mention to anyone." He pulls out his wallet and hands the wide-eyed man a thick wad of bills.

"Not a word," the man agrees as he hurries away.

I give Will a soft smile. "You plan for everything."

"I had some time this morning to consider the options," he replies.

I give him a kiss before we tie the last piece of rope on the final deck chair raft. "I hope these hold."

"They should," he says. "I think we've given more people a chance."

"I wish we could do more." I fight tears as I look out at the ocean, wondering if the iceberg is in sight yet.

Will wraps his arm around me. "As do I. Let's get to the bow. Starboard side, correct?"

I nod. "Yes." We hurry to a spot where we're most likely to see the iceberg strike–if it still does. I hope the guys in the crow's nest have their binoculars. The ocean seems so calm and still. It's so eerily peaceful that I almost nod off in Will's arms as we wait.

But my eyes open just in time to see it, at the exact moment a bell rings in the crow's nest. "There!" I shout, pointing, and Will's wide eyes follow my finger. We run to the railings, and I feel the ship shudder, reverse, and then try to make a hard left turn, but it's just not fast enough. We slam into the iceberg, and Will grabs me to hold me steady as pieces of ice shoot onto the deck.

"Are you all right?" he asks as he steadies us.

I nod, hearing the horrifying sound of the ship running its side along the length of the piece of ice. I'm wide awake now, and Will takes my hand firmly as we run inside to our cabin and burst into Edward's room. I run through to get Agatha, who steps out of bed fully clothed, and we all exit to the hallway.

"Be careful," I say as I hug them both.

"You as well," Agatha says. She pauses for a second as though trying to find the words. "I'm proud my brother has a woman like you."

Tears pour down my cheeks as passengers come out of their rooms. "What's the commotion out here?" one man asks.

"The ship has hit an iceberg," Will says hurriedly. "The decks below are already flooding." Gasps erupt throughout the hallway, though some people just look angry.

My nerves rattle as I realize they don't believe him. But we can't wait, so we run outside with Edward and Agatha, who go directly to a lifeboat. No one is loading them yet, so they stand nearby, waiting. The crew still hasn't received the message yet that they need to load the boats.

A few moments later, we see members of the crew scurrying around. Then, an office rushes over to the lifeboat and directs a crew to get it in place to launch. Agatha gets into the boat, but Edward stays off to the side.

An officer seems to be in charge. "It's women and children first." Only a handful of women and children have materialized, and I have a firm understanding as to why so many of the lifeboats weren't launched at full capacity. No one believed the boat would sink until it was too late.

Will and I encourage the people coming out of the ship to get on the lifeboat. Many of them are still hesitant, but something about the tone of my voice spurs them on. "It's going to sink!" I tell them. "Better safe than sorry!"

After a few moments, the lifeboat fills up, but there are no more women and children nearby.

"Lightoller?" Will says, attracting the officer's attention.

I don't wait, running up to him. "Please fill it up with the men," I beg him. I wave to the wide-eyed passengers standing nearby. "Everyone, please get in."

"But it's women and children first," Lightoller argues.

"I know that," I tell him. "But there aren't any more women and children nearby, and you need to launch this one so that you can move to the next lifeboat." I take a hurried step closer to him, looking into his eyes. "We both know you're going to run out of time."

He blinks a few times and then shouts. "Anyone else then!"

Edward is the only one who reacts. He climbs inside and sits next to Agatha, though I can tell by his expression he's more than a bit ashamed to be doing so. Still, he knows his sister needs him.

The rest of the men seem to pause. "Everyone," I insist. "We need to fill this boat before it can be lowered. Quickly, please!" That seems to get the rest of them moving. A few more women and children come out and climb aboard, but there's plenty of room for everyone standing nearby.

Lightoller gives the order, and the crew begins to lower the lifeboat over the side of the ship.

Will and I give Edward and Agatha's hands a last squeeze. "Take care of one another," Will tells them.

"We will!" his brother and sister both promise. We have to let go. For a moment, we watch them disappear down into the darkness off the side of the ship, and then, we have to move.

Will and I run below decks. "Out, everyone!" Will shouts as we pass people. "Get on the lifeboats!"

We hurry down the outside stairwell, where there is no guard on duty. I see why as soon as we descend the last stairway.

The gate is already locked, and people are pushing on it, trying to wiggle it loose. Roger rushes up to it, pushing through the others with the key in hand. "Let me through! I have a key" he shouts, and people move aside to give him access to the gate.

"Roger! Where's Katie?" I ask.

"She's assisting others," he explains quickly. People flood out the gate as he flings it open, and Will and I lean against the wall to let them pass. I grasp Will's hand firmly in mine.

"There's already water in our room," Roger adds.

"Go straight to the lifeboats!" I yell at everyone as they pass. "Don't wait for instructions. Just get on board. You deserve to be on them just as much as first class!"

The people nod and some stop to thank us quickly before we all hurry up the stairs. I watch Roger race back down below deck and hope he finds Katie soon.

But there's no time to wait. Will leads me back upstairs toward the deck where we made the rafts, pulling them out for people to see. They look pretty rickety, but at least there will be something when all the lifeboats are full.

I catch a glimpse of a boat being launched, thrilled to see that there's not an empty seat in sight. With the help of all the crew guiding it, it lands safely in the water.

We didn't stop the *Titanic* from hitting the iceberg, but I hope this time, many more lives will be saved.

25

"How long has it been?" I ask. With everything happening and so many people running around screaming, it's hard to keep track of the time.

Will pulls out his pocket watch. "One hour. So, we have another hour before she goes down?"

I nod, wishing we had more time than that. "I think we have time to help more people down below."

"I'd prefer that you get on a lifeboat immediately, but I don't believe I'll be able to convince you of that," he says, gazing at me hopefully.

"Absolutely not." I give him a weary smile, which seems ridiculous with everything going on, but there's nothing normal about anything right now.

He nods resolutely. "I expected as much. Well, lead on." He takes my hand firmly. "But I'm not allowing us to get separated."

"That's fair." I don't want to let go of him, either. I feel like he's the only thing connecting me to the world since my reality is so strange right now.

We head for the main stairwell, but so many people are flooding up it, it's impossible to push back against them. I'd rather not impede anyone's progress anyway. So, I go with plan B and lead him to the grand staircase and head down. I know at some point there will be a 'crew only' door that takes us farther down into the ship.

Will moves closer to me, putting his left arm around me protectively while still grasping my hand firmly with his other hand. I pull my skirt up, careful not to miss a step and trip as we head down. I have no idea what deck we're on, but we soon run out of stairs and look for doors that might lead us down further.

When we reach one of them, and I pull it open, several rats run out. Usually, I'd scream and run the other direction with such nasty creatures coming at me, but it just makes my heart race faster with panic while simultaneously making me sad.

"There are a lot of animals on the ship," I say as I run down the next flight of stairs. "They won't make it." I wonder how many of them are in cages screaming in panic right now. I know several people had pet dogs that didn't make it off alive.

Will squeezes my hand tighter but says nothing.

"I know there's nothing I can do for them," I add. "We just need to get to as many people as possible." I try to get the horrifying thoughts out of my mind while running down the hall at the bottom of the stairs.

"Anyone need help?" Will shouts as we reach the third-class rooms. There's no time to open every door, but we fling open a few of them and don't find anybody.

"Let's check the dining hall." To get there, we run through a couple of inches of freezing cold water that's already flooding the hallway. It's getting hard to walk as everything tilts, and with creaking noises echoing from every direction, I know the ship is already starting to sink.

Will opens the dining room door. I gasp a little at the sight of the tables and chairs already starting to float. It's getting bad quickly.

"Anyone in here?" he yells. No one answers, and the creaking and moaning of the ship is getting louder.

"Help!"

There's no one in the dining room, but the faint cry comes from somewhere to the right. Will and I look at each other for a split second then run toward the cry.

A woman clings to her baby in the hallway, and my heart almost leaps out of my chest. "Ma'am, you need to go upstairs," I tell her, putting my hand on her shoulder.

She shakes her head frantically. "I can't find me husband," she says in a thick Irish accent. "I won't leave 'im."

"He's probably looking for you and your child," Will says. "The best thing you can do is make your way to the upper decks and get on a lifeboat."

"We'll look for him," I promise her. "What's his name?"

"Finn." I can see the panic in her eyes, and it tears me apart.

"Okay, we'll look for Finn," I say. "But you and the baby need to get upstairs and get on a lifeboat."

She looks around hopelessly. "I... I don't know the way."

I take her by the shoulder as we wade through the calf-high water to get to the other hallway. "Go straight down this way," I explain. "The door on the end says crew only. Take that and go up the main staircase."

"But I... I cannot read!"

We waste no time leading her to the right door. The water isn't as deep here, but it's rising. "The grand staircase is right that way." Will points through the open door, steering her in the right direction.

"Thanks to 'ya," she says hastily. "Please find Finn!"

"We'll go look for him now." Once she's made it to the stairway with the baby, Will and I run back down the hall and look for her husband, or anyone else who may still be around. We open more doors, look in more rooms, and head down more hallways, making sure I remember which way we came so we can get back. The water continues to inch up slowly but surely.

Finally, Will opens a door to see a man sitting on a bed, his hands covering his face. He looks up hopefully as we enter. "Orla?"

"Are you Finn?" I ask hopefully.

"Aye."

"You need to get on a lifeboat right away," Will says firmly. "Your wife and child have already gone to the upper decks."

"Orla and Aine are well?" He still isn't moving very fast, and I just want to pull him up off the bed and toward the stairs.

"Yes, and you have to go be with them." I guess he just got so turned around and panicked looking for them that he can't think straight. "Please hurry."

Will finally pulls him up and out the door, down the corridor to the partially flooded hallway that leads to the exit. "That open door on the end down there—it leads to the staircase. Run!"

Finn seems to snap out of it and runs out.

"May I take you upstairs now, please Millie?" Will begs me.

I can see in his eyes he knows the answer is no. "We've got to check this other hall."

He doesn't hesitate, holding firmly to my hand while we go a different way toward another hall with passengers' rooms. We throw open as many doors as we can.

"Anyone here?" I shout desperately.

"There's one last hallway with rooms," he says. "Then we need to get back upstairs ourselves."

I nod, not disagreeing now as we hear more creaking, as well as the sounds of things breaking and crashing coming from every direction. The water is above my knees.

Running down the last hallway, we open all the doors until we reach one at the end and find an elderly couple holding each other in bed.

"You need to get upstairs," I insist.

They shake their heads, and I see the terror in their eyes.

"Please, I know you're down in third class, but everyone is getting on lifeboats," I explain. "You can get on one, too. You deserve to survive this just as much as everyone else."

They both look at me blankly, and the man shakes his head, murmuring something I don't understand.

"They don't speak English." Will turns to me. "We need to show them how to get out." I nod, and he coaxes the man by his arm as I reach for the woman, pulling them up. They're both dressed in nightgowns, and I know they're going to be freezing, but it's better than drowning, and they can cling to each other in the lifeboat for warmth. We lead them down the hallway, and they finally catch on and go faster as we show them the escape route. Will points to the grand staircase when we get through the crew door.

Tears fill my eyes as I watch the man, who is frail himself, help his wife up the stairs. I hope they get to a boat in time.

I turn to Will. "One more time."

Will hesitates, and I know he doesn't want to risk it, but he locks his fingers in mine and silently leads me back down the hall and toward the rooms anyway. We check a few final rooms as the water creeps up our thighs. We don't see anyone else, so we head back, reaching the hall just as the ship tilts suddenly. Will grabs me and holds me steady, but the hall in front of us is filling quickly with rushing water.

"This way," he says, holding my hand firmly as I run after him in the other direction.

My dress is getting so wet, it's too heavy and is slowing me down. I start to rip it off and he helps me, then we join hands again and start running, which is a little easier in just Will's pants and shirt.

But a locked gate blocks our way. We have no more keys. Frantic, I turn to him for guidance.

He's not panicked yet, which reassures me. "Let's go down here," he says, and we head down another hall. Finding another door that says crew only, he opens it just as the ship lurches again. He holds me steady, but when I look back, I see a flood of water coming straight toward us.

He pulls me and I run as the wave gets closer and the water beneath us gets deeper. There's a gate in front of us, but thankfully it's half open, and he waits for me as I squeeze through first and pull him with me, reaching the stairs ahead just in time for the gush of water to completely flood everything behind us.

I keep my hand clinging tightly to Will's as we run up the stairs. They're now filled with rats scurrying up just as desperately as we are, and I'm sure I step on more than one as I leap up two stairs at a time. We nearly get knocked down every time the ship starts to shift, so we stop a few times as he holds on and steadies me.

The haunting sounds of breaking wood and steel send shivers of fright across every nerve in my body. But we keep running, finally reaching the top and bursting out onto the promenade.

We both look around frantically. "I think we're too late," I say as he leads me toward the railings looking for lifeboats. The deck is full of people, some screaming, some frozen with fear, and others like us looking frantically for a way off. It looks like all the boats are gone.

"Let's try the other side." Will pulls me gently sideways, and I run after him, desperately looking for a lifeboat that hasn't been launched yet.

But looking around, I don't see any on this side, either. All I can see are the panicked people left on board. Turning toward the ship's bow, I see nothing but icy cold water creeping in our direction.

The bow is almost completely submerged.

We're in big trouble.

26

Will

"Oh, no," Millie says. It's almost a whisper, yet I hear it over all the screams on the deck. I follow Millie's gaze to the ship's bow, which is already underwater. The eerily haunting sounds of steel buckling under pressure have become louder, the ship's tilt steeper.

I have only moments to help her escape.

With no lifeboats in sight, I look into her eyes, my heart aching at the fear in them. I have to protect her and get her off this ship safely, somehow. She has helped save so many people tonight, selflessly insisting on going back down below decks time and again to be sure everyone has a fighting chance.

Yet, I fear for her fate. For her to perish after all she has done for others would be a travesty I cannot accept. I care not what happens to me, but I must find a way for Millie to survive.

I can't help but hope she somehow disappears forward in time to 2025 without ever having to experience being submerged in the frigid ocean water. Though my heart would rip into shreds were she to go, at least she would be safe, back with her family on a much safer version of the death trap we're currently on. I wish I had believed her sooner. I wish I had been more insistent with the captain about the iceberg dangers. Or perhaps I could have insisted that Millie step off back in Ireland while I handle the sinking myself.

Whether I will ever have time to consider my missteps, I cannot know. Now, my attention must be on saving Millie's life, whatever the cost to myself.

"We'll need to look for the deck chairs," I tell her.

One glance at her face, and I can see that even now, she is not just afraid for her own life. She had hoped to avert the disaster altogether, sparing every life on the ship. Yet, we could not achieve that goal, and the ship is going down. Even with full lifeboats, I know from my conversations with the crew that there were not enough to handle every man, woman, and child aboard.

Some will perish. I cannot allow Millie to be one of them.

"Yes," she agrees. "We have to find something to float on before the lights go out. After that, the ship will break in two and go down quickly. We're running out of time."

"This way," I say, keeping my firm grasp on her hand while pulling her toward the stern. Without the moon to light up the night sky, the starlight appears brighter, but I know it will be difficult to see in the shadows when the lights go dark. So, we take advantage of them for now as we run toward the deck where we left the makeshift chair rafts.

Though the lifeboats rowing away look quite full, I'm shaken by how many people are still aboard. It is truly overwhelming to see so many souls fearing for their lives. Their reactions to the loss of lifeboats are heartbreaking.

A mother near us calls out desperately to the disappearing lifeboats. "Please wait!" She clings to the small child in her arms, a young girl around two years old.

I can see Millie's heart break as much as mine. We both know none of the lifeboats will return, even for a woman and child. If they were to try, so many desperate passengers would scramble to climb aboard, it would topside the boat, sinking it. I do not envy the crew in each one for the horrible task of rowing away against the sounds of all these begging souls. But the people onboard their lifeboats depend on them.

"Follow us," Millie tells the mother. "We'll find a way off."

With a mix of hope and fear in her eyes, the woman nods and follows behind us as we move across the deck. It's more difficult to make our way with the mother carrying her child, but Millie keeps an eye out behind us to ensure the woman is still close by.

We weave our way through people as though they are statues in a museum. This takes some effort, as most are frightened into a state of shock. Others are running in circles in panic. Many of those are screaming uncontrollably, unable to find a clear head to focus on finding a way to escape.

I'm horrified to see that a few of them are children, their parents clinging to them desperately.

"Follow us," Millie repeats to as many as she can.

My heart lurches at each one who obeys, as the more people she saves, the harder it will be to get something big enough for all of them to float. Though I wish to save them all, Millie is my primary concern. I will ensure she survives, no matter what.

We pass a lone child who appears separated from his parents, a young boy around the age of Tommy and James, our shuffleboard partners. For a moment, I think of them and pray they're already onboard one of the lifeboats.

"Come with us," Millie says gently. She takes his hand with her free one, and the boy follows.

Now, we move even slower, having to dodge all the people on deck with the three of us joined and several parents with children following close behind.

I force myself to focus on the task at hand. We must find something buoyant. We can't locate any of the rafts we'd made from deck chairs. I hope those have all been put to use and that they save someone's life, yet I fault myself for having not set one out of sight for Millie. I also wish I had convinced her to stop searching the lower decks sooner, but I know she could not have lived with herself had she not saved all the lives she could.

So, now I look frantically in what's left of the ship's dim lighting for anything that will float.

"There!" Millie calls out, pointing with the hand that's still holding onto the boy. "One of the collapsibles is still tied up!"

I waste no time running toward it with Millie and the boy, hoping all the people behind us can keep up. There are a few fathers in our group, and I call out to them.

"Position yourselves on all sides," I shout to everyone, pulling out my pocket knife from my jacket. "There, there, and there. Hold tight. When I cut it free, it may be hard to maneuver, and this ship may shift violently." Though made of canvas and cork, I fear cutting it loose will make it unwieldy.

"Please hurry," Millie tells the men as she takes her place by the boat. Understandably, many of the men are in shock and not thinking clearly, having been awoken from their beds to the disaster many did not anticipate.

Three men and Millie take positions, and I start cutting away at the rope with my knife, immediately regretting that I did not have a larger and sharper one. The ropes are unexpectedly thick, and my sawing motion does not help.

"Try stabbing it and slicing off bits at a time," Millie suggests.

I nod and attempt it, which seems to work, but it's quite time-consuming. "Anyone else have a knife?" I ask. They all shake their heads, their eyes fearful and helpless. Of course, they're all in their bedclothes, hardly prepared with the tools to make an escape from a sinking ship.

Finally, I get through one of the ropes. "Hold here," I tell the man next to me. The ship is starting to rock more violently, with water lapping up onto the deck with each lean. I rush over next to where Millie is holding the boat and work on the rope next to her.

"I'm getting the hang of it," I assure her, but she has no panic in her eyes, nodding and holding steadfast to the boat.

I'm just through the second rope when the lights go dark, and screams erupt from every direction. They blink back on for a moment before going dark again. It takes a moment to even find Millie's face next to me, though it's a comfort when my eyes finally adjust.

"Will, we only have a minute or two!" Her voice gives me a chill, and my heart begins to pound faster than I thought possible. I still have two more ropes to cut loose.

Loath to leave Millie even for a span of three feet, I hurry over to the next rope regardless, struggling to see in the dim starlight surrounding us. I get through it quickly and move to the last one. The ship lurches, sending a giant wave off the starboard side toward us. Desperate to get to Millie, I let go of my knife just as it slits through the last bit of rope.

"Now!" I shout. "Everyone, flip the boat over!"

In the darkness and confusion, two of the men try to flip it in the opposite direction to the rest of our efforts. "To the left!" Millie yells. "On the count of three... one... two... three!"

Everyone heaves the small boat, which falters as it acts like a sail against the strong waves now regularly washing toward us.

A horrifying screech followed by the sounds of splitting and breaking echo through the near darkness.

"Get in!" Millie cries, helping the boy first, then the woman with the baby climbs inside. There's no time to load the boat onto the davits or even to attempt to lower it overboard. Our only chance is that the waves separate us from the vessel before the entire ship goes under.

"It's breaking apart!" Millie yells over the screams of everyone on deck. "Get in!"

Immediately, people start to obey her, and I fear her seat will get lost in the shuffle. I lift her up and place her inside the boat myself, settling next to her and holding her tight. I know it will not be easy to stay in the tiny boat with the pressure of the *Titanic* pulling her down. I hope to be washed clear by the next big wave.

With thankfulness, I recognize Millie's no longer fighting me, resigned to having saved as many people as she could. In seconds, the lifeboat is full, and its occupants brace themselves.

But the crowd nearby notices our tiny boat, and soon we're surrounded by people, all of them trying to get in and shoving others aside.

I cling to Millie protectively, praying she survives this.

27

Millie

"Let me in!"

I can't even tell where the panicked cry is coming from. There are so many people surrounding our little boat, there's no way we can fit them all. But they try to come in anyway, sitting on top of the people who followed us and helped us get it unattached.

"Take my boy, please!"

Will holds me tightly, acting as a barrier between me and the desperate people crowding into the boat. I see the little boy, and I grab him along with the boy who couldn't find his parents earlier, leaving it to Will to keep us in our seats despite the crowd.

"Daddy!" the little boy screams, fighting against me, but I hold him tightly.

"When they get you to safety, tell them about your aunt Beatrice." I look up to see the man standing beside the boat. He's not trying to get in. All he wants is for his son to be safe. His eyes lock on mine for a second, and I see all his emotions in them—gratitude, fear, and helpless acceptance. I nod solemnly as he gives his boy one last hug.

But the ship below us is sinking fast. I can feel it.

"Push off!" Will shouts, and I turn away from the boy's father in time to see a wall of water coming at us as the part of the ship we're on sinks further. Some of the men on the boat help as Will pushes us away from the deck, which is completely underwater now, and launches our little boat into the cold, dark ocean.

"Daddy!"

The boy's father is gone in an instant, along with most of the people who were struggling to get in, and even a few who were already sitting inside have fallen out in the turmoil.

We swirl around as if in a whirlpool, and it feels like the whole boat is going to tip. Screams come from every direction, and I cling to the two boys as hard as I can while Will holds me steady. Finally, the motion subsides enough so that Will grabs an oar and starts rowing us farther away from the ship, toward the other lifeboats I can make out in the dim starlight. I can't get to the other oar to help with so many people sitting in the way, but one of the men on the other side manages to pull it out, so we get farther away.

Once we are away from the dark shadow of the Titanic in the distance, we reach a group of people floating in the water. Many of them are still screaming, and I feel some of them hitting the side of the boat while others are pulling on it, trying to get in. One rather large man grabs the side and attempts to lift himself up, heaving the lifeboat in his direction. Now that we're actually floating, it's easier to tell how much capacity it has, so I feel confident we can add more people, but not if they're going to capsize us.

"Stay low and hold onto the side here," I instruct the boys. "I need to help these other people." It'll be easier for us to pull people inside than for them to try to climb in. Both boys nod, their eyes wide, and the one who just lost his father is crying. But he follows the other's lead, and they both cling onto the side together.

"We have to bring in more people," I tell Will, but he's already doing that, having put the oar down nearby as he reaches down to pull people in the water into the lifeboat.

"Grab my hand!" I yell at a woman who is flailing around near me, but she doesn't seem to be listening. "My hand! Take it!" I yell louder, and that seems to get her attention.

She's close enough that I can pull her if she just gets a hold of my hand. But instead, she puts her arms back in the cold water to start paddling. I can tell she's too panicked to save herself, so I reach for her, leaning over the side of the boat. I grab her freezing cold hand and grip it as hard as I can, but I soon realize I've leaned way too far. In her panic, she tugs my arm, and I start to lose my balance. The world goes sideways as I fall straight for the icy water. I brace myself, trying to hold onto the boat with my other hand, but I don't want to let go of her, and she refuses to let go of me.

My heart thumps wildly in my chest.

I'm close to the water when I stop falling, feeling Will's strong arms around my waist pulling me back. Once I'm safely inside the boat, he takes hold of the woman's arm, and we both hoist her up and into the boat. She's so cold, and her clothes are so wet I don't know whether she'll survive the night, but I need to grab onto the next person and hope just being close to all these other people in the lifeboat will help keep her warm.

We get a man up next, but it isn't easy as he's a lot heavier and seemingly paralyzed with fear since he's not helping us lift him. I'm surprised he has kept himself above water in this state. I pull as hard as I can, but it's mostly Will who gets him up over the side of the boat and inside. Two of the men on the other side of the boat are also pulling people in, and the boat stays surprisingly buoyant. We can fit several more, I think, before we need to worry about staying afloat.

So, Will and I reach for the people nearby. The next one is an older man, and I can tell he's getting tired. Will manages to grip his shoulder, but he's a little too far away from the boat. He starts flailing his arm around, and Will loses his grip. There's no way to get him back as he floats farther away. I feel like I can't breathe, knowing we're losing him, but there are people being pulled aboard on the other side, so we can't row over to him. It's a grim thought to know that we can't save everyone.

I lose sight of him when a woman swims up to us, and Will easily grabs her, and we get her on the boat. My heart aches for that poor man. I can't imagine how he's feeling knowing he's going to die.

"We need to move further from the ship!" Will shouts, getting the oar out again.

I can feel, rather than see, what he means. We're getting stuck in a whirlpool current again, so more of the *Titanic* must be going under. We need to get as far away from it as we can, or we won't have saved any of these people. A man across from me grabs the other oar and starts rowing along with Will, and we make some progress getting out of the swirling water. We get further away from most of the people in the water in the process, which means we won't be saving anyone else, but there's nothing else we can do.

My heart pounds even stronger now, and every nerve in my body is on edge.

Once we stop, I look around. My eyes have adjusted better to the starlight, which seems almost bright with no moon. It's eerily silent for a moment, and I see some people attempting to swim toward us. They aren't making much progress because the water is so cold. I guess they've reached the point where screaming has to be replaced with saving themselves, for those who have the strength, at least. The screams seem distant now that we've pulled away.

I'm glad that there aren't as many people in the water as I expected from everything I've learned about the disaster, from the movie and all the documentaries I've seen. I catch sight of two other lifeboats nearby, and I can see they appear very full, though people are still shouting toward them, asking them to come back.

Will stops rowing and sets the oar down again, wrapping one arm around me protectively. I meet his eyes, and it feels like my heart skips a beat. "I love you, Will." I have to say it again now in case this is the end for me in this time. Whatever I was supposed to do here, maybe it's done. I don't know how I got here, but I've known the whole time it can probably happen in reverse as well.

"I love you, Millie," he whispers.

I open my mouth to say more, but the horrifying screeching and crashing makes us both turn toward the *Titanic*. We watch in horror, our hearts pounding, as the ship lifts up into the air as the front goes down, dragging the back half back down hard onto the surface of the water. I see the outlines of bodies being flung free from the deck as more screams fill the air, and then the shadow slides beneath the ocean, sinking into the abyss.

The world goes silent for a heartbeat as time seems to stop, all of us frozen in shock and terror.

And then the screaming resumes.

This time, it's coming from the water and the lifeboats, including ours. People in the boats wail in despair at their loss—husbands, wives, children, friends. I can't even imagine the devastation they feel. In the water, people are screaming for help, desperately trying to stay afloat.

And in an instant, several of them reach our boat. Will and I start grabbing for them again. Some of them are reaching up for help, but others are clamoring to climb up its sides, and I realize it might tip. I reach for the two boys to push them toward the middle of the boat as people start trying to climb in right by me, at least three or four of them, all pushing the boat down. In the process, Inside the boat, people are shouting that we need to row away, that it's too much. Too many people.

Will picks up an oar and begins to try to row through the sea of bodies. I know he doesn't want to, but it's the only way to save those of us already on board.

We begin to put a bit of distance between ourselves and the crowd when suddenly I feel a hand reaching over from the icy depths of the water. It's a large man. I stare down into his horrified, round eyes, seeing icicles forming on his mustache. He tugs on me, surely hoping I can help him get on the boat.

Instead, I lose my balance again, and this time, Will is too busy rowing to see it in time. I yelp as I fall head first into the icy water, the man letting go of me as soon as I am of no use to him. I feel what has to be Will's hand on my arm as I go under. It's too late. I slip from his grasp.

Every nerve of my body feels like it's being stabbed with a knife, shocking my system for a moment as I go completely underwater. I fight my way back to the surface, raising my head to see Will's horrified expression as he reaches for me, shouting my name. I try to lift an arm toward him, but the boat's moving so far away, and I'm already beginning to stiffen from the frigid water.

I want to tell him goodbye, that I love him, that I'll miss him... but my mouth won't work. I gulp down a mouthful of icy sea water and then slide beneath the surface again. The world around me goes black.

All the screaming around me goes silent, except for a single splash next to me. I think I feel someone grabbing for me, but that sensation disappears soon too.

The only thing left is the icy cold and a deep, penetrating blackness that surrounds me.

2 8

Millie

It feels like just seconds before the darkness starts fading. In fact, it becomes much brighter than it should be in the middle of a moonless night in the ocean, and I have to close my eyes tighter. What's even stranger is that the cold has faded, and I think I feel the sun on my skin, but that's impossible. I fell into the icy Atlantic in the middle of the night wearing Will's clothes.

Turning to the side, I let out a cough. I sputter a few times and crack open my eyes for a moment but have to close them quickly. It doesn't feel like I'm wearing Will's clothes. In fact, it feels like I'm wearing that itchy bathing suit.

How....

"She's awake!"

I swear it's my sister's voice, but it can't be. Feeling a shadow over my face, I open my eyes, blinking to adjust to the light. The first thing I see is Will's beautiful eyes. "Will...."

"What's that?" It's definitely my mother's voice, and I turn to see her run over and kneel next to me, wearing the same swimsuit and coverup she'd had on when she'd tried to take a picture of us.

"Mom?" I keep blinking, the haze in my mind not quite registering any of this.

"Thank God you're okay," she says, stroking my forehead. "We were so worried when we couldn't find you."

"Couldn't find...." I scoot up onto my elbows and try to sit up, feeling a hand helping me. I look back at Will and furrow my brow. Nothing about his touch is the same. When I meet his eyes, I understand why.

It's not Will.

Instead, it's the young man I'd seen in the pool area earlier, the one with mesmerizing blue eyes. They're a lot like Will's but not quite the same without the intensity of that dark outline of the iris... and missing the love for me.

My heart rips to shreds. He's gone. I'm back in 2025, and I'll never see Will again. Maybe it was all just a dream that filled the moments I was blacked out from falling into the pool. Maybe my mind had just taken that handsome young man with the blue eyes and made him into the perfect man of my dreams.

But it all felt so real. *How could it not be real?* Tears well up in my eyes, but I try to blink them away. Two people I thought I'd never see again are right next to me—my mom and sister. Ally and the young man help me to my feet and guide me over to the table where Mom put all our things. My phone is right in front of me, but I don't pick it up.

"What happened?" I ask, rubbing my head. It hurts the way it did when I first woke up on the real *Titanic*.... Well, maybe that part wasn't even real, but it's so strange that the pain felt so genuine in a dream.

"You slipped and fell," Ally explains. "I saw you hit your head and go in the water, and I jumped in after you. But you weren't there."

My brows furrow again. "What?"

Mom sits next to me. "We'd better have the ship's doctor look at that."

"She's on her way." I turn to see a crew member I've never met. "I think it's best we stay here until she has a look at her before we walk her all the way down to her office."

"I agree," Mom says. "Honey, does it hurt?"

"Yes, but—" I still feel so fuzzy. I look at Ally. "What do you mean, I wasn't there?"

She shrugs. "Like seconds after you fell in the water, you were gone. I mean, I jumped right in. You just weren't there. It was like you'd disappeared and went to another dimension or something."

I hitch a breath.

"That's ridiculous, Ally," Mom says. "Of course she was there." She looks at me. "Your sister probably panicked, and you were just lower in the water than she thought."

"No, she was gone," Ally insists. "Like disappeared, gone, poof, no Millie."

"Stop that." Mom gives her an annoyed look and turns back to me. "Anyway, thank God this young man was there. He jumped in and saved you. You might've drowned if not for him."

I guess I should thank him, but even looking at him reminds me of Will. And with what Ally said, maybe I did disappear, and for that split second here, I was actually back in 1912 for several days.

Maybe it was all real.

I'm so confused. I turn to him anyway, trying to breathe despite the huge lump in my chest. It's so heavy and painful, so much worse than the lump on my head. As my mind clears, I become pretty sure Will was real, and that he's gone forever. I really don't know how I'm ever going to cope with that. "Thank you," I say softly.

He nods and smiles. There's something in it that makes him look more like Will, but it's just a coincidence, not the real Will I left somewhere in the Atlantic Ocean in 1912. *Did he survive?* I wonder if history will be different now. More people survived if what I went through was true. The lifeboats were full. Maybe I'll find his name in some records somewhere.

"I need to go." *Titanic 2* is full of historical information about what happened. Some of it must have changed in all the exhibits aboard.

"No, you don't." Mom nudges me back down into the chair. "The doctor's here, and she needs to look at you first."

"I'm Dr. Carter." I look up to see a woman smiling sympathetically at me, holding a black medical bag. For a moment, I think about how amazing it is that a woman can be a doctor now, or whatever she wants to be. "Let me have a look, okay?"

I nod, leaning back and letting her look at my head. A bump on my noggin is the least of my worries. How am I going to live without Will?

She does a few tests, having me follow her finger with my eyes and whatnot. "I'm fine," I insist.

"It seems that way," she says with a nod. She turns to my mom. "We'll need to watch for a concussion. Do you know the signs?"

I don't listen to her answer, looking down at my hands and thinking about Will. I already miss him so much, but there's nothing I can do. I don't know how I managed to travel through time, but I know in my heart I'll never be able to do it again. I feel so lost and alone, even with Mom and Ally right beside me. My heart belongs to a man who's alive over a hundred years ago.

It's all so hopeless.

But I'm forced out of my thoughts as we all turn toward the sound of splashing around in the pool. Two strong arms emerge on the side, fully covered in a drenched black suit. I hitch a breath as the man pushes himself up, breaking the water's surface and shaking off his head.

He leans against the side for a moment as he looks around, his deep blue eyes landing on me.

Will....

He's here!

Is this real?

Some people rush up to him, including the young man who looks like him, who lowers an arm to him to help him up. I scramble to stand, but my mom stops me with a firm grip on my arm.

"Millie, what are you doing?" she asks. "The doctor isn't finished with you."

I shake my head. "I'm fine." I look at the doctor, hating to peel my eyes away from Will in case he disappears again. All I want to do is close the distance between us. "I'm okay."

I don't wait for her answer, standing and pushing around her as politely as I can, dodging other people gathered around as I make my way toward the pool. I catch Will's eyes again, and my heart flutters. Relief fills me, and every nerve tingles with excitement.

The closer I get, the bigger his smile grows. The few seconds I'm running toward him feel like forever, but finally, his arms open, and I rush into them, not even caring that he's soaking wet as I bury my face in his chest. He holds me tight, and it's as if time stands still for the moment.

"How?" It's all I can say.

"I have no idea." It's so comforting to hear his voice as he whispers softly in my ear. "But I'm here with you."

"Um..."

I pull back from the hug, but not completely, and see Ally standing there, her face half smiling and half confused.

Mom is next to her. "You know this man?" Her brows are knitted tightly together, and there's not a hint of a smile on her face.

"Yes," I say, realizing immediately I have no excuse for knowing this gorgeous man from 1912 who just stepped out of the ship's pool. "He's a... a friend from school."

"Hmm."

"I promise I'm fine," I insist. "I'll be right back." I lead Will by the arm away from the crowd, where he takes off his jacket and hugs me again. I can explain it to Mom later... or not.

"I can't believe you're here!" I give him a squeeze before pulling back so I can look in those gorgeous eyes again. I want to kiss him, but that can wait. "But I have no idea how you did it." For that matter, I have no explanation for my change in clothing either.

He shrugs, his smile wide. "Perhaps by the same method that brought you to me to begin with." He glances back at the pool. "So, it's true what you said about the outdoor pool."

I laugh, squeezing his hand. "Yes." But then I realize he's left his own family behind. "Are you okay? Edward and Agatha—"

"Will be just fine," he insists. "They were some of the first to get in a lifeboat. I'm confident they will make it to the rescue ship."

"Yeah, that's true. But you'll miss them."

"I'm simply glad to be with you," he adds, his eyes glistening. "I made a wish that I would get to come with you, and here I am."

I bite my bottom lip and smile at him, feeling like I'm bursting at the seams with happiness. I'm back, and Will is here. I don't know how this happened, but my heart is soaring.

"Excuse me."

We turn to see the young man again. Will's eyes go wide for a second but soften, filled with understanding. Something seems to pass between them, and I look back and forth.

"What is it?" I ask.

"Maybe we should talk privately," the man suggests. "I have a dry outfit waiting for you in my room."

I tilt my head with confusion, but Will takes my hand, and we follow him. This man seems to know something about us, and I want to find out why.

29

Will

So much has happened so quickly, I feel like I'm in a whirlwind. It was only moments ago that I was reaching for Millie's hand in the cold, dark ocean. I was so angry with myself for moving away from her for a moment to row us away from the crowd that I didn't realize so many people were attempting to crawl on board right by her seat.

Going from that horror to suddenly being in a crystal clear, bright pool, then finding her safe and in the arms of her family, wearing the same swimsuit I found her in on the *Titanic*, has all been so profoundly overwhelming, it feels surreal. Yet, here she is beside me, her warm hand in mine as we walk down the hallway of this brightly lit ship.

As we follow what should be a stranger down the hallway, I feel comforted by how much he looks like me—and my brother. I think back to the arrangement I made with Edward before the original *Titanic* sank and hope this is that plan coming to fruition.

He leads us to a stateroom, entering first. I keep Millie's hand firmly in mine, though I still don't anticipate any malicious intent from this man.

"I'm David," he says when we're inside and the door is closed. "Will, right? And you must be Millie."

He smiles as he opens the closet, and I turn to Millie, who is staring with wide eyes. "How do you know our names?"

"I've been expecting you," he says as though the explanation is clear. "I wasn't sure how you were going to get here, though. But boy, do you make an entrance." He chuckles as he pulls out a change of clothing. His eyes flit between me and Millie. "I guess I'd better explain a little more. My great-great grandfather is Edward Stewart."

He looks me square in the eye, and I nod in understanding. I turn to Millie, whose wide eyes have turned from confusion to excitement. "Edward survived!"

"He did," David says with a firm nod. "And your sister, Agatha, too. I have a lot to tell you, but maybe you'd rather get changed into some dry clothes first." I take the clothes from him as he nods toward a door. "Bathroom's in there. You should probably change while I get out a few things. I have a package for you."

I don't want to leave Millie, and thankfully she follows me into the bathroom. It's small, but there's enough room for both of us. I finally have a moment to kiss her, and I take advantage of it. Her lips feel so warm against mine. To have thought I almost lost her was too much to bear.

We pull apart after a brief moment.

"He's waiting out there," she says with a giggle. "You'd better get dressed. Then we'll spend the rest of forever together."

"Now, that is a phrase that warms my entire soul."

I can't keep the smile at bay as I unbutton my shirt and take it off. I do the same for my pants, and Millie gives a low whistle. "You'd better put these on quickly."

I laugh as I put on the unusual underwear and then the pants she hands me, which have a strange fastener in front.

"It's a zipper," she explains. "Hold this part out and pull it up, then push it in at the top." It works surprisingly well. The shirt pulls over my head, and though it's tight, it isn't much different from my swim-suit that sank along with the *Titanic*.

"Wow, you look even hotter in 2025." She wiggles her eyebrows, which I find charming, and though I don't completely understand the phrase, I catch its meaning well enough.

We open the door to find David sitting on the bed next to a box. "Ha, I was wondering how long I'd have to wait. I promise, I'll give you some privacy in a few minutes. But I'd better give you the rundown first."

I'm a bit confused at his language, but I approach as he opens the box. "Here's the letter from your brother."

The note is contained in some sort of smooth, see-through mater-ial, yet it's still readable.

"My Dear Brother Will,

I hope this letter finds you well and that you and Millie are reunited in her time. Agatha and I were received on the *Carpathia* in good health, though she was understandably shaken. We received word from those in a collapsible lifeboat that both you and Millie were aboard, but both of you fell over the side and never resurfaced. Some young boys that were with you said you seemed to disappear beneath the water. I believe in my heart that you are alive and well in 2025, and so I will keep the promise I made to you that night on the ship.

We settled in well with our grandparents, and both Agatha and I have found love in our new home, America. My wife is expecting our second child at the date of this writing, and Agatha is doting over her son, William, at this very moment. Know that we have full lives thanks to you and Millie, who saved us both from certain death in that cold ocean.

I've prepared separate written instructions for our children to pass to their children, and so on, until the year 2025 occurs, and one of them will meet you on that ship where Millie first disappeared from her family. I trust whoever is with you now will provide you with everything you need.

Agatha and I love you dearly, my dear brother. May your future with Millie bring you as much happiness as we continue to enjoy thanks to you.

Love always and throughout time,

Edward."

As tears begin to pour from my eyes, I see that Millie is sharing the same sentiment. "She named her baby after you," she chokes out through happy tears.

"Apparently so." I give her a smile.

"Man, this is so wild," David says. I look up, having almost forgotten his presence. "You really did come here from 1912. Some in the family didn't believe it, but I always did. Anyway, I got you some things. It's amazing what you can get when you grease a few palms."

He chuckles, and though I don't understand completely, I watch as he pulls more documents out of the box. "So, this is your birth certificate," he explains. "Says you were born in 2001. That's three years before me!" He looks proudly at us. "Just had my twenty-first bash the other day."

"Happy birthday," Millie says.

"Yes, happy birthday to you." Some of what he's saying is confusing, but again, I get the gist of it.

"Thanks," he says with a toothy grin. "Anyway, I guess they calculated based on your actual age. The day is the same, just a little tweaking of the year." He chuckles. "And we have your college degree here. That was a little harder, but we got it done. Also, your driver's license... I posed for the picture."

He grins again, and I just shake my head with amazement. This is so much at once.

"Everyone's driver's license photo sucks, right?" he asks.

Millie laughs and seems to understand. "Cars are a little different now, so I'll teach you what you need to know."

I nod. Just being in the world with Millie is enough. I'll adjust to whatever is needed.

"Okay, the last thing is the house," he continues, handing me what must be a set of keys, but they look so different from what I've experienced. Apparently, I have a lot to learn. "The deed is here. Your brother bought it way back when, and we've kept it up. Did a few renovations just last year to make it more modern. I hope you like it."

"Where is it?" Millie asks.

"Out on some acreage near your hometown," he explains with a grin.

"We can be close to my family?" Her smile is so beautiful.

"Yep." He pulls out a large folder that looks full of documents. "Oh, I almost forgot the finances. We'll just say you don't need to worry much. Sizable bank account, stocks, bonds.... Some of our ancestors still had to guess at a few things, but when cell phones first came out, they knew that was a good investment. Oh, and we got you a phone too."

"This is all so amazing," Millie says. "I don't know how we can ever thank you."

"Well, invite me to the wedding, and we'll call it even," he says. "We're family, after all. Right?"

"You can stand in as my best man," I promise.

Millie smiles wide. "Though he hasn't proposed yet."

"I guarantee you I will very soon," I say quickly. "Allow me time to prepare for it properly once we're at home."

She lets out a giggle. "I'm sure you'll make it good."

"There are more letters in here," David explains, pointing to the box. "I'll just leave this all with you. I guess you two have a lot to talk about, so I'll get out of here. I'll be back to get ready for dinner though. Don't worry, I'll knock."

Millie giggles and gives him a hug. "Thank you again. I guess I'll never stop telling you that."

I offer my hand. "It's a pleasure to meet you. I trust we'll spend a lot more time together before this ship arrives at her destination."

"You bet," he says. "Have fun, you two."

When he closes the door behind him, I take Millie into my arms and kiss her deeply. She relaxes into the kiss, wrapping her soft arms around me as I melt into her.

"Wow," she says when we part. "This is all so amazing. He prepared for you to come back all this time. And Edward and

Agatha… I'm glad they never gave up on you. They could have just as easily thought you were lost at sea."

"Most definitely," I agree. "My brother is… was, quite special."

"He'll always be in your heart," she says, running her palm along my chest.

"Right now," I say, reaching up to stroke her soft cheek, "I'm more concerned about what's in your heart."

She giggles softly, her beautiful green eyes sparkling. "You know my heart belongs to you, and that's all I want to think about right now. After all, we were destined to be together."

I smile at her in agreement. "Until the end of time."

EPILOGUE

Three Years Later...
Millie

My eyes are barely open as I feel Will's strong, warm hand against my cheek. "Good morning," he says, leaning in and bringing his lips to mine.

"Mm," I moan between tender kisses. "Good morning."

"Did you sleep well?" He pulls back a bit, propping himself up on his elbow next to me.

"Not bad, considering." He rubs my belly tenderly. "It's getting pretty uncomfortable. This pregnancy is a lot different than the first time. I just want the day to come so we can hold them both."

"Just a couple more weeks to go," he says cheerfully. I love the look in his eyes these days, just full of pure happiness.

"What?" He chuckles lightly.

"Nothing... well, not nothing." I start to push myself up into a sitting position, and he helps me, adjusting the pillows. Every movement is becoming a big deal. "I worried for so long that you'd miss your family, even though you always say you're fine."

"I am fine," he insists.

"I know, but sometimes you must think about Edward and Agatha."

"Every day." He rubs my belly again and gives a chuckle, laying a light kiss on my lips.

"Not those two, silly." I run my fingers over his hand and around my belly, where our own little Edward and Agatha are growing. "I'm glad we could tell the sexes already so we could name them. You can't always tell, you know."

"The technology of this time still amazes me," he admits. "I'm starting to get used to it, though."

"You sure are. Those last two investments took a lot of research."

"Well, the computer classes when I first arrived in this time paid off." He gives me a smile. "Though, that Mr. Malone couldn't figure out how a man my age needed so much help with such things."

I giggle, pressing my lips to his again before pulling back. "But you caught on fast." My phone buzzes on the dresser. "Speaking of technology...."

"I'll get it," he says after my futile attempt to wiggle toward the edge of the bed.

I smile as he hands it to me, and I read the text. "It's Anne from the museum. The truck will be here at 1:00 today."

"You do realize you're on maternity leave," he says with a chuckle.

"I'm not missing this, though. It's not every day a truck arrives with actual artifacts brought up from the *Titanic*."

"I'm teasing," he says. "Of course you won't miss it. I'm anxious to see some of it as well."

"Well," I say, sneaking in one more quick kiss, "as husband of the director of The Titanic Preservation Society, you will definitely have that privilege." I love my job. I knew as soon as we got back to America what I wanted to do, and with the help of some other very talented people, we got the project up and running.

"I'm thankful to be your husband for so many reasons," he says. "But I can't wait to see if any of it is mine, or if any of Edward or Agatha's belongings survived."

"I hope they did," I agree. "I'd love for you to have more items to remember them by." I look at the time. "And we'd better get up. Katie will wake up any minute, and breakfast is probably about ready."

"I'm on it," he says, and I laugh as he gets up and comes to my side of the bed to help me up. "What?" he asks with a grin.

"You're really catching on to all the modern slang, that's all."

"Well, I plan to live in the modern world for the rest of my life, so I suppose I should get comfortable with it." He helps me swing around to get my legs down and gives me an arm to pull me up. I can't help but remember his outstretched hand years ago—I suppose it was over a century ago now—when he tried to pull me out of the cold ocean.

"Mommy! Daddy!" comes a call from the next room.

I let out a chuckle. "I knew it." Will helps me with my robe and throws on his own before going into our daughter's room.

Katie sits up, her teddy bear in hand. "I hungry."

I smile at our daughter, our first miracle. I found out I was pregnant only weeks after the *Titanic* disaster. Though we'd been intimate almost constantly, so I'm not completely sure, I still like to think that Katie was conceived on the ship, only a few decks above her namesake, the amazing woman who helped us save so many of the third-class passengers, our good friend Katie. I was thrilled to find her name on a survival list, along with her husband, Roger.

The list is so much longer now than the one from before I went back in time. Many more people lived, so I'm happy I could be a part of that. They still changed the lifeboat requirements, though, along with other safety measures, because it would have been a lot better if everyone could have made it off safely.

"Well, we'd better go down for breakfast then." Will scoops her up, and they both look my way with those same deep, blue eyes. Katie has that dark ring around the iris just like her father, but her hair is almost exactly the same shade as mine.

I give our daughter a kiss. "I'm hungry, too!" I've been joking about eating for three for the whole pregnancy, but lately, I'm really feeling that. It's like I'm always starving.

The scent of fried potatoes and bacon hits me as we head downstairs. Having a live-in cook and housekeeper is the one splurge I really love from all the money Will's family set up for him, not to mention all he's been making as an investor since going into business for himself.

"Good morning!" Louise gives us all a warm welcome, but she mostly has eyes for Katie, and that's fine with me. She's been a huge help with our daughter, and I don't know how I would handle adding twins to the mix without her.

"This looks fantastic. I hope you made a lot."

Louise chuckles as she helps Katie into her booster seat. "Don't worry, I did."

I'm almost finished with breakfast when I get another text. "Oh, Anne says she emailed me the manifest. I've been waiting for that." The museum has been working with a crew collecting artifacts from the *Titanic* for the past year, making sure everything was handled correctly to preserve every item. I would have loved to be the one out on the ship overseeing things, but with the twins on the way, I decided not to risk it. The two scientists we sent are more than competent.

Will pauses with his fork in his hand as I pull it up and scan through it. "Lots of dishes in this load, and a few tables. It's amazing that any furniture is still salvageable. Let's see... hmm, lots of jewelry." I scan down the list. "Will... oh, my God!"

"What?"

"There's one lot from your—" I almost blow it and say sister. We haven't told Louise our little secret. I don't want her to think we're crazy, and I know I would if someone told me that. But we have told her Will is a descendant of one of the passengers... sort of. "They're bringing some jewelry from your family's room."

His eyes go wide. "That's fantastic."

I can tell he wants to say a lot more about that, and so do I. We're getting used to waiting until later to talk about it. Katie is almost finished eating anyway, and I need to get her cleaned up. As always, Will is already on it, finishing up his last bite while he stands up and takes the warm washcloth Louise hands him.

"My little girl sure likes bacon," he says as he wipes her mouth and hands.

I let out a chuckle. "I honestly think she just likes playing in the grease."

He laughs as he finishes wiping her hands, helps her down from her booster seat, and leads her toward the living room where we have a toy box full of her favorite toys. I look at Louise, who waves me on, making me giggle. I've given up offering to help her clean the dishes since she always insists I go sit down, especially recently.

My little family runs ahead of me, and by the time I get to the living room, Will is on the floor next to our daughter with a huge bag of blocks.

I walk over to the mantle above our giant marble fireplace where we've displayed photos of both our families. "I'm so glad we found these pictures," I say.

"As am I," Will agrees. Once we had made it to Southampton aboard *Titanic 2,* we'd been able to recover some pictures of Edward and Agatha, as well as his parents, from the historical society there, and we've since had them restored. Along with their pictures are photos of my family, including my dad, and of course, dozens of baby pictures of our little Katie.

With Louise all the way back in the kitchen, I can finally talk about the artifacts. "I hope they found that emerald brooch of Agatha's I wore on the ship. I'd love to hand that down to Katie or our little Agatha one day. I wish the dresses could have made it, but they probably dissolved years ago."

"I'll never forget the way you looked in those gowns," he says with a sly wink. "You took my breath away in an instant, and you still do, to this day."

I make my way over to the couch and slowly lower myself onto it, giving a chuckle. "I hardly look breathtaking right now." I'm sure my face is red from just that effort, not to mention the fact that I still need a shower.

"You are the most beautiful creature I ever laid eyes on," he says, his dark blue eyes piercing mine from his spot on the floor.

My heart flutters as it always does whenever I see love for me in that man's eyes. It's amazing to think how close we came to not being together. I have no doubt fate brought us together.

He looks at Katie. "And I'm the luckiest man in the world to be here with you and our children."

I want to kiss him now. His grins widens as though he can tell. "Daddy will be right back." He puts the block he's holding on top of their very random building project and comes over to the couch, sitting next to me and putting a gentle hand on my belly.

"I love you so much, Millie," he says, his voice deep yet soft.

Tears surface as I look at him.. Everything we've been through together flashes through my mind—the ship, the dancing, the love-making, the near drowning... then our wedding, with my mom walking me down the aisle toward those same beautiful blue eyes, and the moment in the hospital when we both held our daughter for the first time.

"And I love you so much too, Will."

He presses his lips to mine, and I close my eyes. All of those fond memories and heartache has led us here, and I can't wait for what will come next.

We have a love that spans across time, thanks to a ship that sailed the ocean to bring us together... the *RMS Titanic*.

THE END

Thank you for reading! Back to Gettysburg *will be out soon!*

ALSO BY ID JOHNSON

Stand Alone Titles

All I Want for Christmas is Pooch

(*sweet contemporary romance*)

Christmas Memory

(*sweet contemporary romance*)

Meet Cute Me Under the Mistletoe

(*sweet contemporary romance*)

The Doll Maker's Daughter at Christmas

(*clean romance/historical*)

Pretty Little Monster

(*young adult/suspense*)

The Journey to Normal: Our Family's Life with Autism (*nonfiction*)

Found by the Alpha (*fantasy romance*)

Love Throughout Time

(*time travel romance*)

Back to Titanic

Back to Gettysburg

Back to Bunker Hill

Back to the Highlands

Back to Port Royal

Back to the Inquisition (Sept 2025)

Back to Salem (Oct 2025)

Back to Plymouth (Nov 2025)

Back to Whitechapel (Dec 2025)

Back to the Old West (Jan 2026)

Back to the Ton (Feb 2026)

Back to the Crown (March 2026)

Back to Pompeii (April 2026)

Silverwood Academy

(paranormal romance)

Vampire Hunter

World Builder

Realm Jumper

Celestial Springs

(psychological thriller/literary fiction/women's fiction)

Beneath the Inconstant Moon

The First Mrs. Edwards

Leaving Ginny

The Motherhood

(dystopian romance)

Rain's Rebellion

Rain's Run

Rain's Return

Ashes and Rose Petals

(contemporary romance/retelling of Romeo and Juliet and Cinderella)

Girl in the Attic

Girl From the Tomb

Girl On the Beach

Nashville Country Dreams

(contemporary romance)

Meant to Marry Me

Lead Me Home

You Are the Reason

Forever Love series

(clean romance/historical)

Cordia's Will: A Civil War Story of Love and Loss

Cordia's Hope: A Story of Love on the Frontier

The Clandestine Saga series

(paranormal romance)

Transformation

Resurrection

Repercussion

Absolution

Illumination

Destruction

Annihilation

Obliteration

Termination

A Vampire Hunter's Tale (based on The Clandestine Saga)

(paranormal/alternate history)

Aaron

Jamie

Elliott

Christian

The Chronicles of Cassidy (based on The Clandestine Saga)

(young adult paranormal)

So You Think Your Sister's a Vampire Hunter?

Who Wants to Be a Vampire Hunter?

How Not to Be a Vampire Hunter

My Life As a Teenage Vampire Hunter

Vampire Hunting Isn't for Morons

Vampires Bite and Other Life Lessons

Gone Guardian

Death Does Not Become Her

Blood of the Vampire Hunter (based on The Clandestine Saga)

(paranormal romance)

Night Slayer

Shadow Stalker

Queen Catcher

Mother Hunter

Father Finder

Ghosts of Southampton series

(historical romance)

Prelude

Titanic

Residuum

Lusitania

Heartwarming Holidays Sweet Romance series

(Christian/clean romance)

Melody's Christmas

Christmas Cocoa

Winter Woods

Waiting On Love

Shamrock Hearts

A Blossoming Spring Romance

Firecracker!

The Clandestine Saga Books 1-3

The Chronicles of Cassidy Books 1-4

Celestial Springs Collection

Heartwarming Holidays Sweet Romance Books 1-3

Heartwarming Holidays Sweet Romance Books 4-7

Websites: https://books2read.com/ap/xX7ZD8/ID-Johnson

For updates, visit www.authoridjohnson.blogspot.com

Follow on Twitter @authoridjohnson

Find me on Facebook at www.facebook.com/IDJohnsonAuthor

Instagram: @authoridjohnson

Follow me on Bookbub: https://www.bookbub.com/authors/id-johnson

Printed in Dunstable, United Kingdom